From Megan Maitland's Diary

Dear Diary,

Less than a year ago, I despaired of ever seeing my brood settled, and suddenly they're falling like flower petals. A mother's prayers answered!

Anna, bless her, may put a stop to my run of success, however. She defines the "once burned, twice shy" maxim. I've seen her give men a longing glance, then turn away as though convinced she'll never find happiness in a relationship and has decided not to even try.

She uses her son, Will, as an excuse, but I think he should be her <u>reason</u> to round out their family. He's brilliant, all right, but he's still a little boy. His uncles do their best to give him their attention, but now they have wives and are planning families of their own. Will needs some kind man's undivided attention.

Isn't it ironic that Anna's been hired to plan Austin Cahill's wedding, when he's just the man whose business genius my stock-market-savvy grandson holds in such awe? I consider the man quite a catch myself. <u>Sigh!</u> If only Anna could have gotten to him first! But now I'm getting greedy. Even a mother can't have everything!

Dear Reader,

There's never a dull moment at Maitland Maternity! This unique and now world-renowned clinic was founded twenty-five years ago by Megan Maitland, widow of William Maitland, of the prominent Austin, Texas, Maitlands. Megan is also matriarch of an impressive family of seven children, many of whom are active participants in the everyday miracles that bring children into the world.

When our series began, the family was stunned by the unexpected arrival of an unidentified baby at the clinic— unidentified, except for the claim that the child is a Maitland. Who are the parents of this child? Is the claim legitimate? Will the media's tenacious grip on this news damage the clinic's reputation? Suddenly rumors and counterclaims abound. Women claiming to be the child's mother are materializing out of the woodwork! How will Megan get at the truth? And how will the media circus affect the lives and loves of the Maitland children—Abby, the head of gynecology, Ellie, the hospital administrator, her twin sister, Beth, who runs the day-care center, Mitchell, the fertility specialist, R.J., the vice president of operations, even Anna, who has nothing to do with the clinic, and Jake, the black sheep of the family?

Please join us each month over the next year as the mystery of the Maitland baby unravels, bit by enticing bit, and book by captivating book!

Marsha Zinberg,
Senior Editor and Editorial Coordinator, Special Projects

MURIEL JENSEN

Billion Dollar Bride

TORONTO • NEW YORK • LONDON
AMSTERDAM • PARIS • SYDNEY • HAMBURG
STOCKHOLM • ATHENS • TOKYO • MILAN • MADRID
PRAGUE • WARSAW • BUDAPEST • AUCKLAND

HARLEQUIN BOOKS
225 Duncan Mill Road, Don Mills,
Ontario, Canada M3B 3K9

ISBN 0-373-65069-8

BILLION DOLLAR BRIDE

This edition published by arrangement with Harlequin Books S.A.

® and TM are trademarks of the publisher. Trademarks indicated with ® are registered in the United States Patent and Trademark Office, the Canadian Trade Marks Office and in other countries.

Visit us at www.eHarlequin.com

Printed in U.S.A.

Muriel Jensen is the award-winning author of over sixty books that tug at readers' hearts. She has won a Reviewer's Choice Award and a Career Achievement Award for Love and Laughter from *Romantic Times Magazine*, as well as a sales award from Waldenbooks. Muriel is best loved for her books about family, a subject she knows well, as she has three children and eight grandchildren. A native of Massachusetts, Muriel now lives with her husband in Oregon.

To David Charbonneau and Diane Dezielle
and our special connection.

CHAPTER ONE

ANNA MAITLAND turned in the swivel chair at her desk to keep Caroline Lamont in sight as she paced the lavender and cream office.

"I see a medieval English theme," Caroline said, her voice hushed as though she were describing a vision. "Ivy-trimmed bowers, costumed knights, the wedding party dressed appropriately and arriving on horses."

Anna smiled and nodded. When a Wonderful Weddings client planned to "perform" rather than be married, there was little she could do but give her what she wanted. Anna had always considered fulfilling dreams her business, but her work wasn't half as much fun when a client insisted on making it "theater."

"And when we turn around to leave the church," Caroline went on, "I'd like butterflies to be released!" Her voice rose a little in her excitement over the idea, and she spread her arms wide to suggest a cloud of monarchs fluttering around her.

"I'm afraid I can't provide that, Caroline," Anna said, continuing to smile.

Caroline came to sit on the edge of Anna's desk. She was tall and coltish and absolutely gorgeous. She had chin-length dark blond hair framing gray eyes that widened or narrowed with the intensity of her mood. It was early April in temperate Austin, Texas, and she wore a casual sweater and pants the color of early-blooming lavender crocuses.

"Sure you can," she said, her glossy lips curving in a smile. "They're the rage now. I think you get them from a nursery or something."

Anna nodded. "Or an insect farm. They're shipped overnight in a special, refrigerated container, individually boxed for each guest. You can do that if your heart is set on it, but you'll have to make the arrangements, and you'll have to accept delivery and handle every part of it."

Caroline blinked in apparent mystification. "They don't sting or anything. There's no need to be afraid of them."

It was difficult for Anna to maintain a serious look. She hadn't expected to like Caroline Lamont when they'd been introduced at Maitland Maternity Clinic's twenty-fifth anniversary party last month. Caroline had a reputation in the press and among Texas society as a fun-loving party girl who enjoyed her family's oil money. Her sister, Camille, worked hard for charity, but from all indications, Caroline did nothing worthwhile but appear front and center at every social event Texas had to offer.

Anna had expected a frivolous snob. But Caroline seemed to be more of a frivolous nice person. Eager to indulge herself, she was nonetheless pleasant and courteous, seemingly unaware that there was a world outside the rarefied one she occupied.

"I'm not afraid of butterflies," Anna said patiently. "But I could never do anything that would result in one being put in a box."

"But they're not hurt. They fly away."

"Would you like someone to put you in a box, just so that when you stepped out of it, you'd look pretty for that person?"

Caroline considered a moment and did not appear to find the idea disagreeable. "I suppose it would depend upon who was opening the box." She smiled thoughtfully then shook her head. "Guests could toss rice or birdseed instead, but that's so mundane—not to mention messy."

"What about flower petals. They'd be in keeping with your theme, I think."

That pleased her. Then she asked gravely, "Do you think we'll have to go to London for the armor and the costumes?"

Anna struggled with her expression again. She'd indulged many extravagances in the years that she'd been in business, but she'd never traveled out of the country to outfit the wedding party.

"I...think we can find everything we need here," she said. "I know Mr. Cahill has given you a considerable budget for the wedding, but think of the fun you'll have shopping on your honeymoon if you conserve a little here and there."

Caroline batted that notion away with a pen she'd picked up off Anna's desk. "Oh, there'll be no real honeymoon. Austin and I aren't a love match. Everyone knows that. We're going straight to his place on Kauai after the wedding to make a baby."

Anna stared at her. "Really," she said.

"Really." Caroline waggled the pen between her thumb and forefinger as she explained. "He's one of the richest men in Texas, you know, and I don't know what brought it on, but he just got to thinking one day that he had no one to leave everything to. He has a mother, but that's it."

"He's never been married?"

"Never. He can't take his mind off business long enough. Anyway, we've been friends since we met at a Junior League dinner three years ago. We both have a lot of money, and neither one of us believes in love. Austin was jilted by his fiancée a couple of years ago when she used her position in his company to help a rival firm take him over." Her grim expression suggested Cahill's reaction. "They failed, but since then, he's had it with women."

"But what about you? Don't you want love in your marriage?"

Caroline smiled wryly and shook her head. "I had parents who took vacations without me and regularly forgot my birthday. But that meant I could do whatever I wanted, and I rather like that now. I'd hate to have to change for someone. So our arrangement will be perfect. No one interferes with our lives."

"Marriage," Anna suggested mildly, "will interfere with your life." It had almost ruined hers, but she kept that to herself. "A baby will play havoc with it."

"All I have to do is produce the baby." Caroline shrugged gracefully and looked around the office, as though happy with her lot in life. "Then I can stay or not, depending on how I feel. The baby's for him."

Anna continued to stare at her in disbelief. "You probably don't understand this now," she said, "before it's actually happened to you. But you won't be able to carry a baby for nine months, deliver it, then just go your merry way."

Caroline nodded with a gravity Anna found both distressing and sad. "I will," she insisted. "I don't stick to anything. Not school, not work, not friends. Austin's the longest relationship of any kind I've ever had. I don't know how to do them, so it's easier not to try."

Anna felt desperate to reach her. She'd had a loveless marriage herself when she'd been Caroline's age, and it had shaken something deep down, some belief in the world's underlying goodness, in the nobility of man.

She'd been able to go on, even to be happy again, because she was part of a large and wonderful family. But she'd been changed forever.

And she'd carried and delivered a baby. She knew walking away would not be as easy as Caroline imagined, despite her claims of never having known love.

"Are you sure you want to do this?" she asked, putting a hand to Caroline's knee. "For a man to marry a woman solely for the purpose of creating an heir to a fortune is medieval!"

Caroline laughed musically and pinched Anna's fingers, the serious moment erased. "That's what gave me the idea for the theme!"

"Ms. Maitland?" The office door opened, and

Eden Ross, Anna's part-time secretary and occasional baby-sitter, peered around it, her dark eyes wide and her cheeks flushed. "Mr., um, Austin... No, no," she corrected herself, her usual high-school-senior sophistication wobbling precariously. "That's his first, um...Mr...."

"Cahill," a helpful male voice offered quietly from the other side of the door.

Eden closed her eyes in mortification, but she regained her professional demeanor. She drew a breath and squared her shoulders. "Mr. Cahill is here for Ms. Lamont."

"Show him in, please." Anna smiled to let Eden know the occasional slipup was never fatal. The girl was smart, responsible and determined, but she took herself too seriously.

When Eden pushed the door open, Anna immediately understood her confusion.

A tall, well-built man walked in and unconsciously took control of the room. The quiet, feminine office with its striped silk wallpaper, lavender carpet and Hepplewhite desk took on a decidedly masculine mood.

In a finely tailored gray suit that covered broad shoulders and long legs, he walked to Caroline's side. He had dark brown hair cut very short, blue eyes the color of dusk, a strong, straight nose and a jaw that probably won him arguments before he ever said anything.

Anna felt as though she should stand—not out of courtesy, but because the room suddenly hummed with energy and sitting down seemed unacceptable.

Besides, he was worth a bundle, and his fiancée was apparently determined to spend a significant portion of it on a Wonderful Wedding. Anna rose as Caroline began introductions.

"Austin, I'd like you to meet our wedding planner, Anna Maitland," Caroline said as she stepped comfortably into his arm. "Anna, this is my fiancé, Austin Cahill."

"I'm pleased to meet you, Mr. Cahill." Anna extended her hand, feeling small. It wasn't just his size, she decided as he told her with a brief smile that the pleasure was his. It was his stature, a sort of presence that said, *I can do anything, and I'm different from other men because of that.*

She couldn't help but wonder while her hand was swallowed in his why such a man would find it necessary to make a deal with a woman to get a child.

AUSTIN CAHILL would have given anything not to have to deal with all the fuss and feathers that went with a society wedding. But Caroline had agreed to his unorthodox request to give him a child, and the least he could do was give her the wedding she wanted.

He could afford to be generous today, anyway, emotionally as well as financially. He'd just made a deal for prime land outside of Austin. Eventually the site would accommodate a mall that included an indoor children's playground in an atrium, a library, conversation areas and athletic courts for bored husbands. Several of his peers had laughed at the notion, but he had faith in his plan.

One day his child would inherit a fortune in nine figures. He took great pride in that knowledge.

His child, he thought as he glanced around an office that looked like an eighteenth-century drawing room. Would he sire a boy or a girl? It didn't matter, really. The child would be made up of his genes, and that just about guaranteed a good business head.

He wrapped his arm more tightly around Caroline, grateful she was willing to be part of such an unusual marriage. And for her "beautiful" genes, which their child would undoubtedly inherit.

She hugged him briefly and he held on, ignoring the small pinch of disappointment that tried to cloud his vision at these moments. They were good friends. He felt great affection for her. She didn't *want* love from him. So why did his heart insist on reacting to the fact that it wasn't there?

They had fun together, enjoyed each other's company, but whenever they touched, he got that pinch, and though it didn't deter him, it unsettled him.

"I'm telling you, Austin," Caroline was saying, "we are *so* lucky to get Anna. She has a dozen other clients right now, but she's taking us on because she and Camille worked together on that project for the hungry. You remember? We went to the dinner."

And because she's going to charge me a fortune, he thought, *to fulfill all your wild ideas. She'll probably be able to retire on what you have in mind.*

He reached across a small desk to shake hands with this paragon. The woman was strikingly beautiful, if a man had a preference for brunettes. Personally, he'd sworn off them since Lauren. It was a senseless prejudice, he realized, but since he'd been unable to see what was inside his former fiancée and protect himself from her deception, it was a sort of defense mechanism to stay away from women who had her outward appearance.

Still, this woman had none of Lauren's petite fragility.

She was five-seven or maybe five-eight, with a woman's maturity in her breasts and hips. His mind took her out of the silky white blouse and cranberry suit and put her in black lace. Accustomed to Caroline's slender, leggy proportions, he'd forgotten how much he'd once appreciated roundness in a woman.

She had eyes the color of dark ale, and rich, deep brown hair, bundled up in a knot at the back of her head. It was side-parted and glossy in the sunlight shining through the window, and he could imagine how glorious it would look if she wore it loose.

This was the kind of woman who should bear a child, he thought. One who seemed all warmth and soft curves.

Then he noticed that the expression in her eyes was pitying and sad. That snapped the moment back into place.

"Ms. Maitland," he said, drawing his hand away, erasing his previous thoughts. "The pleasure is mine. Carrie has some pretty wild ideas. Do you think you'll be able to accommodate them?"

She nodded. "All except the butterflies."

He'd been against that one himself, though he hadn't said much about it. He didn't want to do anything to discourage Caroline from going through with their arrangement.

"We can manage without butterflies," he said.

"Good. Then I'll contact a costumer and an armorer first thing tomorrow."

He wasn't sure he'd heard that correctly. "An armorer?" he asked.

"For the knights who'll line the entrance to the church," Caroline said.

Knights? "I thought you had a Regency period theme going? Carriages, maypoles…"

Caroline shook her head then rolled her eyes indulgently. "I told you about it last night in the limo, but you were reading stock reports and probably didn't even hear me."

He had to do better in that regard, he knew. He did tune her out sometimes because she tended to go on and on about details in which he really had no interest. He wanted a marriage in order to have a baby, but he didn't care at all about the wedding.

"We're doing medieval." Caroline hooked an arm in his and winked at Anna. "I was thinking it'd be more dramatic, more exciting. We're bound to get a couple of pages in *Vanity Fair*."

"And that's a goal of ours?" he asked wryly.

"I think it's a given, darling. Austin Cahill is marrying Caroline Lamont. Two stars of Texas royalty getting hitched. Nothing cliché, nothing less than first class. Everything magical."

God, he hated this. But he made himself smile. "Well, I'm sure you'll make it spectacular. But…where are we going to find new armor?"

Caroline shrugged. "That's Anna's job. And afterward you can put it in the garden or something. Or I can take it with me. They're bound to make spectacular conversation pieces."

He had to grant her that. "Okay. Are we finished here?"

Caroline turned to Anna. "Can I call you as I get ideas and come up with questions?"

"Of course." Anna handed Caroline a business card. "This has my cell phone, my e-mail and my fax."

"Great." Caroline tucked the card in a tiny lavender bag slung over her shoulder. Austin always wondered what was in there that could be important enough to carry around and still be small enough to fit in the four-by-four-inch space. She turned to him and giggled. "Anna thinks *you're* medieval."

Austin was surprised to learn that this beautiful woman had any opinions about him. But he was interested, also. "Have we met before?" he asked Anna.

She'd closed her eyes at Caroline's statement, apparently in dignified mortification. She obviously hadn't known Caroline long enough to learn that she expressed aloud every thought that came into her head.

Anna opened her eyes, and with a sigh and a fatalistic smile, she replied, "No, we haven't. I..."

"She wanted me to save money on the wedding," Caroline said, laughing, "so we could go shopping on our honeymoon, but I told her about our arrangement."

He didn't know why he should feel embarrassed in front of a wedding planner. Most of his close friends and several of his staff knew why he was getting married—they'd even suggested Anna as a consultant. Some praised his practical approach and others told him they thought he was crazy, but none of them had looked at him with such condemnation in their eyes.

"I didn't realize," he said a little stiffly, "that you were concerned with the reason for a wedding. I thought your job was to insure everything goes smoothly."

She nodded, as though she'd expected him to say just that. "You're right, of course," she agreed. But before he could feel too righteous about having put her in her place, she added quietly, "I guess I thought the face of a woman being married solely for the purpose of producing a baby might reflect a less than joyful expression as she walked down the aisle. There should be something blue at every wedding, but it's not supposed to be the bride."

Smart-mouthed and quick. Not necessarily desirable qualities in a woman. Particularly when he couldn't think of a comeback that wasn't rude.

Then Caroline came to his rescue.

"So I explained that I was doing this willingly," she said, squeezing his arm, "and that there was no problem."

"Thank you, Carrie." He turned a look on Anna intended to intimidate. "I assure you I'm not a villain, Ms. Maitland. But I realize you know nothing about me. Perhaps you'd prefer not to..."

"I know a lot about you, Mr. Cahill," she said,

clearly unaffected by his glare. He must be losing his touch. "You went to Harvard on a scholarship and hold a master's degree in business administration. You'd made a million dollars in the hotel business by the time you were thirty and added mall development to your ventures, along with a few odds-and-ends companies like..." She narrowed her eyes as she obviously worked to recall a name. "Gordon Maps and Books," she finally said with a little smile of triumph, "and Bronson Builders. Today you are the head of a multibillion-dollar company, Cahill Corporation, and—" she sniffed the air and smile devilishly "—your fragrance is Brooks Brothers."

He was more fascinated by her knowledge than annoyed by her one-upmanship. "You read *Forbes?*" he asked. The magazine had done a piece on him several months before.

"My son does," she replied. "You're his idol."

The compliment took him by surprise. "Me?" he asked incredulously.

She nodded, a soft light coming into her eyes. "Will is ten, and he isn't into athletes or rock stars, but business moguls. He intends to be one himself one day."

He had to laugh. "Good for him. I had a lucrative lawn and garden care business going when I was ten."

"He takes care of my sisters' and my stock portfolios," she said, "and has formed a Fuzzy Buddies clearinghouse for his friends so they can buy, sell or trade to keep their collections complete."

"Fuzzy Buddies?"

"Those little plush toys everybody's collecting," Caroline said in clarification. "I've got the flamingo hanging from my rearview mirror." She turned to Anna, her eyes bright. "That's so *cute!* You should meet Anna's son, Austin. The little guy would probably love that!"

Austin tried to imagine a ten-year-old boy being as enthused about business as most kids that age were about sports, but couldn't. Anna Maitland was flattering him for the sake of his business.

But she did know all about him. Maybe she'd read the *Forbes* article?

"There's a lot going on while we're here, Carrie," he said. "And I am trying to run a business by remote control."

"But you can make time." Caroline frowned at him.

He tried to usher her toward the door. "I'm sure I'd prove to be a disappointment in person."

"Austin..."

"So you can work with us, Ms. Maitland," he asked, pulling the door open, "even while offended by the reason for our marriage?"

Anna followed them to the door, and Caroline stepped into the hallway. "I wasn't judging, Mr. Cahill," she said. "I was just offering an opinion. And if *you're* offended by that, you might want to hire another consultant."

"I have no problem with other people's opinions," he said, "when they relate to business. But I don't like interference in my personal life."

She held the door while he passed through it. "It

was an opinion on Caroline's life. She is the bride, after all, and seeing that the bride has everything she wants on her special day is my job."

"Good," he said. "You take care that she has everything she needs for the wedding, and I'll worry about her mental and emotional well-being."

No large undertaking, he knew. Caroline had shut off her deepest feelings long ago, and her mental well-being was just fine because she skimmed along the surface of her emotions fearful of rekindling the ones she'd disconnected.

He could see from the expression in Anna Maitland's eyes that though she might not know the details, she'd already grasped the obvious about Caroline.

With a patronizing subservience he didn't trust for a moment, she inclined her head.

"You'll have a wonderful wedding," she assured him, stepping back through the doorway as Caroline led him toward the elevator. "And Caroline will be a beautiful bride." She waved at Caroline, then closed the door to her office.

He wanted Caroline to be the bride all women dreamed of being so she would never feel that she'd sacrificed anything to give him his baby.

They stopped to wait for the elevator.

"My word!" Caroline exclaimed with a shake of her head. "Are you two going to argue until the moment I walk up the aisle? Why is her opinion so important to you?"

"It isn't. I just didn't want her upsetting you."

"Oh, we were just talking, one woman to another. Don't worry about it. I know what I'm doing."

"But are you happy about what you're doing?"

She shrugged noncommittally. "I'm never happy, you know that. But I agreed, didn't I? I have nothing going on for a year or so. We may as well make a baby."

He felt that pinch again and gave the down button an impatient jab. Why did he want her to be happy, he wondered, when they didn't love each other? It didn't make sense.

"And I'm not upset," Caroline went on. The light over the elevator blinked its arrival and a buzzer sounded. The doors parted on an empty car and they stepped inside. "In fact," she said as the doors closed, "I'm pretty excited about the prospect of a medieval wedding."

She smiled at him coaxingly. "You can ride a horse, can't you?"

Austin forced himself not to shudder.

CHAPTER TWO

"MOM! WHERE ARE YOU?"

Will always came through the office door shouting for her, just as he did at home. The school bus dropped him off outside the building, and he did homework in a corner of her office until they went home together.

She sat behind her desk, in plain sight, not ten feet from the doorway in which he stood. She'd often wondered if his father's absence made him want to keep close tabs on her.

"Right here in front of your face, Will," she said, gesturing him to come to her. "Where else would I be?"

He dropped his backpack on her desk and wrapped her in a sturdy hug. She relished it, knowing that the next ten years would pass with the speed of the last ten and he'd soon be in college somewhere thinking about business and women and forgetting to give his mother the time of day.

She studied him as he drew away and leaned against her desk, his white sweater smudged and his jeans muddy at the knees. He had her dark hair and eyes, though he'd inherited his father's aristocratic nose and chin. He wore wire-rimmed glasses and a usually serious air, though he did have a wry sense of humor and a sunny smile. He smiled at her now.

"You're always saying that one day Michael Keaton's going to come and take you away to the Batcave. I thought he might have come while I was gone."

"As if I'd leave for the Batcave without you. Did you eat all your lunch?"

"Except for the carrot sticks I traded to Ashley Bates."

"Traded for what?"

"A cupcake."

Anna groaned. "Will, I try to balance your lunch so that you get all the nutrition you—"

"Mom," he interrupted reasonably, "if someone wanted to give you a cupcake for your carrot sticks, you'd have to be brain-dead not to make the deal. It was like getting Microsoft stock for railroad shares."

Anna laughed and hugged him again. He was the best thing in a life filled with pretty good stuff, and she never took that for granted for a moment.

"What did *you* have for lunch?" he asked, falling into her client's chair.

"Caesar salad with shrimp."

"Ah. Austin Eats again, huh? I know it's only across the street, Mom, but you're in a rut."

She nodded and pushed to her feet. "And if you don't mind digging yourself in there with me, I noticed they had chicken and dumplings on the dinner menu." It was one of his favorite meals—and the cook-housekeeper's day off. "Want to eat there tonight?"

"Please. Anything's better than those frozen chicken and spinach calzone things we had last week." He crossed his eyes and made a terrible face. "Even your cooking would be better than those."

She chased him to the elevator.

AUSTIN EATS was a small diner with a circular counter in the middle of the room and square tables and chairs all around. It served fifty or so customers and was busy for every meal and most times in between.

Framed photographs of local events lined the pale yellow walls, and a large bulletin board behind the cashier was a rotating gallery of new babies, birthday-party photos and postcards from vacationing patrons.

It was like eating at home surrounded by friends and not having to cook.

Two glasses of ice water were placed on the table the moment Anna and Will settled in one of the window booths.

"And how are my two favorite customers?" Mary Jane Potter asked with a bright smile. She was in her early twenties and small but buff, her curly brown hair caught up in a casual topknot. She wore her Austin Eats uniform with great style and a very serious-looking pair of athletic shoes. She took a pad and pen from her apron pocket and winked at Will.

"How's my Scully Sports Equipment stock, Will?"

"Up two-thirds of a point," Will replied with a proud smile. "Slow growth is good."

Mary Jane grinned at him. "Then how come you're getting so tall?"

"He's a blue-chip stock," Anna said. "We're here for the chicken and dumplings, Mary Jane. Is Shelby cooking tonight?" Shelby Lord owned Austin Eats.

"No, Sara's cooking."

"Does she make it as well as Shelby does?" Will wanted to know.

Mary Jane scribbled on her pad. "Maybe even better. She must have worked for Wolfgang Puck in her other life. Salads or soup? The soup's tomato rice today."

"Soup!" Will said with enthusiasm.

Anna shook her head. "Neither, thanks. Just some coffee."

"Right. And milk for Will."

"Pepsi," Will corrected.

"Milk." Anna overruled him. "Thanks, Mary Jane."

As Mary Jane left to place their order, Will pulled the napkin dispenser toward him and gave Anna two napkins, taking two for himself.

"I don't need strong bones," he argued good-naturedly while replacing the dispenser. "I'm going to run a big company, not play professional basketball."

"All smart companies today have in-house gyms to help reduce employee stress. Thank you." Mary Jane delivered their drinks and was gone again. "Your employees will expect to see you there."

He grinned. "I'll just show up in the sauna like Uncle R.J." Will looked in the direction of the kitchen, then leaned conspiratorially toward Anna and asked quietly, "Where do you think Sara came from, Mom? I mean, it's weird that she's been here seven whole months and she still doesn't remember anything."

Anna took a sip of her coffee, then shook her head as she replaced the cup. "I don't have an answer to that, Will. No one can say when she'll get her memory back. All we know is that she sustained a head injury that probably caused the memory loss. Even the specialist the hospital brought in from Dallas said she could get her memory back tomorrow, or it could take months. I guess those things are unpredictable."

Sara had wandered into town, dazed and unable to remember her name. She'd been taken to a women's shelter, and Daisy, the director, had brought her to Maitland Maternity Clinic, the hospital run by Anna's family, because it was closer than the hospital across town.

When Sara had finally been declared healthy except for the memory loss, Daisy had pleaded with Shelby to give her a job. Sara had proven to be a good waitress—and a good cook.

She had golden blond hair and blue eyes with a questioning look in them that Anna noticed every time she saw her. It was almost as though she expected a clue to present itself at any moment, a revelation that would answer her questions.

"Imagine not knowing who you are," Will speculated, sitting back in the booth. "Not knowing your mom or your dad or your friends. I wonder how she remembered she could cook."

"Shelby said the cook had a family emergency a few weeks ago and couldn't come in to work. Sara started cooking. It was probably instinctive."

"She just knew she could do it?"

Anna nodded. "That even happens to people who *know* who they are, but don't know what they're capable of," she said, unable to resist making a life lesson out of their serious conversation. "When put to the test, they do things they didn't know they could do."

"Sort of like discovering they have super powers."

Anna was about to nod, but her maternal radar spotted the danger in doing so without qualification. "Internal super powers," she specified. "I wouldn't try to fly or see through lead or anything."

Will rolled his eyes at her. "I know what you mean, Mom. I wasn't planning to leap tall buildings."

"Good." She never knew for certain with him. He was extremely intelligent, unusually gifted, but still a ten-year-old boy. His sense of daring and adventure occasionally overruled his common sense. "I'd just prefer not to have a repeat of the gunpowder incident."

He frowned, distracted by the memory of the experiment that had given her a few of the worst moments of her life. "I still don't understand why that didn't work," he said absently. "According to the book, sulfur and potassium nitrate should have been a perfect launching fuel."

Fortunately, he'd tried to launch a teddy bear and not himself, but in the process he'd blown out the bathroom window and the glass on the medicine cabinet, and ignited the shower curtain. The teddy bear had gone to his reward.

If R.J. hadn't been there, Anna wasn't sure what she'd have done when she heard the explosion and opened the bathroom door to find her son covered in soot and glass and lying motionless on the floor.

Will had come to immediately, and R.J. had gotten the glass off him and out of his hair with a Dustbuster. Then he'd taken him to the emergency room, where they'd found nothing wrong with him except singed eyebrows and hair and rampant inquisitiveness.

R.J. had talked her out of locking Will in his room until college and made an effort to spend more time with him. Even now that R.J. was married, he made Will a part of his life.

Will shrugged off the incident. "I guess it showed that science isn't my thing." He sat back as Mary Jane delivered his soup and Anna's coffee. "Money is."

As Mary Jane left again, he asked seriously, "Do you think I get that from my father? Even though I never see him?"

Anna shook her head, eager to rid him of that notion. "You get it from the Maitlands," she said, pushing the pepper toward him. "Almost all of us are into some kind of business. Besides the clinic itself, there's Lana's baby shop, Shelby's restaurant—" she spread her hands to indicate Austin Eats "—and Aunt Beth's day-care center in the hospital."

"And you."

"Right."

"But Shelby and Lana are Lords," he corrected, "not Maitlands."

Anna nodded, pointing to his napkin to remind him to put it on his lap. He did, then pulled his soup closer and picked up his spoon.

"But we Maitlands sort of think of them as cousins," she explained, "because Grandma found Garrett and the triplets on the doorstep of Maitland Maternity not long after she opened it. She found a loving home for them close by and we had parties and picnics together. Our interests rubbed off on each other."

"I just wonder why he doesn't like me," Will said candidly.

They were back to his father again. Anna preferred not to think about her ex-husband, but she knew that understanding his rejection was important to Will's peace of mind.

"He doesn't dislike you," she assured him quickly. "He doesn't even know you well enough to make any judgment about you. He just thinks of himself first. Life always seems easier if you never have to consider anybody but yourself."

"It must get lonely," Will observed.

She was pleased he understood that. "I'm sure it does. Guess what client I took on today."

He spooned soup into his mouth with enthusiasm, pausing to add more pepper and take a guess. "Um…that lady that's the mother of that baby Grandma has? The one that's your new cousin Connor's girlfriend?"

"Janelle?" Anna shook her head. "Nope. I took

Janelle and Connor on last month. This is a client I officially got today.''

Will shrugged, more interested in eating his soup than trying to guess.

"Caroline Lamont," she said.

"Who's that?" he asked between spoonfuls.

"A nice lady who has a lot of money. But guess who she's marrying."

"Who?"

"Austin Cahill."

She watched with delight as Will dropped the spoon into his empty bowl and stared at her in wide-eyed disbelief.

"Mom," he said gravely, "you're kidding, right?"

She shook her head. "I'm not. They want a medieval English wedding, and I have to find costumes and armor and horses."

His mouth fell open.

"You can help me with that part if you like," she said.

He still didn't believe her. "No way!" he challenged.

"Way," she assured him.

Hero worship blazed in his eyes as he finally realized she spoke the truth. "But...he lives in Dallas!"

"Right. But Caroline lives here in Austin."

"Wow." He pushed his bowl aside and leaned toward her pleadingly. "You think I'll get to meet him?"

She remembered Cahill's resistance to Caroline's suggestion. "He's pretty busy right now," she said gently. "He's involved in getting ready for the wedding and trying to run his business from here."

He absorbed that information, then seemed to dismiss it, as though the notion that he could be this close to his hero and not meet him was unthinkable.

"Did he say anything about the RoyceCo takeover?" Will asked eagerly. Before she could answer, he added, "Did he say what he's going to do about the pet stores in their subsidiary company?"

"Didn't you just buy us RoyceCo stock?" Anna frowned in puzzlement. "I thought it was a grain company."

He nodded. "I bought it because I knew Austin Cahill was looking at it seriously. I think RoyceCo bought a dog-food company as a place to use some of their grain, and those guys had pet stores. Anyway, those stores—I think they're called Dogdom—have been in violation of Texas animal protection laws. Somebody has to make them change."

"He didn't say any—"

"I'll bet that's why he bought it!" Will beamed. "'Cause he heard the animals weren't being treated right and he wanted to fix that!"

Anna was willing to let him believe that. It reminded her again that although her son had a keen, almost adult mind, he was still a little boy. He understood the workings of business, but not the motivations of those who made the deals.

She doubted seriously that Austin Cahill had purchased RoyceCo to see that the animals owned by the subsidiary pet stores were better treated. He was taking a wife for the sole purpose of producing an heir.

With so little regard for a human being, he couldn't possibly care that much about animals. He was in it for the profits in grain.

"Maybe we'll run into him," Will said hopefully, "while I'm helping you with the armor and the horses."

"Maybe. We'll have to find a way to work it out when his schedule loosens up."

Mary Jane brought their dinners, and conversation stopped while Will consumed his, then finished off the second half of Anna's.

"Sara's a *really* good cook," he said appreciatively as he contemplated the last bite. "I'll bet she cooked for the president or somebody."

Anna had to agree that her chicken and dumplings were delicious. The seasoning was perfect, the biscuits light, the mashed potatoes creamy. An hour on the treadmill tonight, she thought, might save her hips from retribution.

"I can stay up late tonight," Will boasted as he pushed his plate aside, "'cause I don't have school tomorrow. Can I have peach cobbler?"

"Sure."

"A là mode?"

"Is there any other way?"

Anna beckoned to Mary Jane, who brought Will's favorite dessert without being asked.

"Aunt Beth wondered," Anna said casually, "if you could help out at the day care tomorrow, since you have the day off."

Will gave her a direct look that changed subtly to one of disapproval. "Mom, I'm on to you. You think if you make me feel like Aunt Beth needs my help, I won't get mad about having to spend the day with a bunch of little kids. I thought I was going to spend the day with Uncle R.J."

She hadn't been able to skate anything past him since he was four. She didn't know why she continued to try.

"It helps her a lot when you read to the little ones," she insisted. "And Uncle R.J. and Aunt Dana have an appointment he'd forgotten when he said you could stay with him."

He looked disappointed. "Why can't I just go over to Eddie's?"

"Because no one's home at Eddie's house."

"Mom, we're ten years old." He said it as though they were twenty-one.

"I know that, Will," she replied patiently, "but I'm more comfortable knowing that you're nearby, and that someone I trust has an eye on you."

"But it's embarrassing to have to stay at a day care!"

"You're not staying there, you're assisting."

"I'll bet Austin Cahill never had to stay at a day care when he was ten," he grumbled, then finished his cobbler in silence.

Anna put an arm around him as they walked to the cashier. "We'll stay up late and scarf brownies while we're watching Leno, okay?"

That earned her a tentative smile. "Okay. But you owe me big for this, Mom."

She squeezed him to her and kissed the top of his head. "I owe you big for a lot of things, kiddo."

WILL LAY on the sofa, covered with a throw, and watched television. Curled up near his feet, Anna checked her source catalogs for the unique requirements the Lamont-Cahill wedding would call for.

She'd made a few notes when there was a knock at her door just after nine. She walked from the family room at the back of her rambling ranch house, through the kitchen, the dining room, then the living room, wondering who would be calling at this hour.

Her brother and his wife stood on the doorstep, their cheeks flushed and their eyes alight with their love for each other.

Anna smiled to herself. That love had come as such a surprise to her brother R.J. As president of Maitland Maternity Clinic, he'd hired Dana as his secretary years ago and had worked closely with the beautiful blonde every day without noticing what had grown between them.

"Hi!" Anna greeted them. "What's up?"

"My hormone level!" Dana replied without trying to ease into the reason for their visit. Her green eyes were alight with excitement. "We're going to have a baby!"

R.J. turned to his wife, laughing. "Oh, that was well done. What happened to 'Let's be subtle and mysterious?'" R.J.'s hazel eyes could often be difficult to read, but tonight they were as revealing as Dana's.

"I couldn't stand it another moment!" Dana cried as she wrapped her arms around Anna. "Oh, Anna. We're so excited!"

"What?" Will demanded, racing to the door in his

Dallas Cowboys knit pajamas, rubbing sleep from his eyes.

"You're going to have a cousin!" Anna exclaimed to Will as she drew his aunt and uncle inside and closed the door. "Well, I'm excited, too! That's wonderful! Have you told Mom?"

"Not yet," R.J. replied. "I wanted to tell you first."

"Will," Dana said, "I hope our baby is half the sweetheart you are."

Will blushed furiously. "Sweetheart?" he questioned, glancing at his uncle.

"Dana means she hopes he's a great guy like you." R.J. shook his head at Dana. "Guys don't like to be considered sweethearts, my love. Only women appreciate that."

Dana hugged Will. "I'm sorry, Will. I mean that in the most complimentary way."

Anna left Will to entertain them while she excused herself to make a fresh pot of decaf.

Even now that they were adults, Anna worried about R.J.'s sense of disconnection from the family.

She and R.J. had been born to William Maitland's brother, Robert, then abandoned when their mother died and Robert left, unable to cope. R.J. had been three and Anna just six months old.

William and Megan had adopted them and raised them with the same love and attention they gave their own children, but R.J. had struggled with the knowledge that he wasn't really their child and that his father had abandoned him.

Though he'd always been protective of Anna, he'd

also thought of her as William and Megan's daughter, because he remembered their natural parents and she didn't.

It was a defense mechanism, she knew. He'd been afraid that genes would win out and someday, despite all his efforts to the contrary, he'd find in himself the same irresponsible qualities their father had shown.

Even after he'd become president of Maitland Maternity, he'd held himself a little apart from everyone—except her—for fear he would fall short of what was required of him.

While Anna loved and counted on their closeness, she worried about the subtle distance he kept between himself and their family.

Now, though, as she heard R.J. and Dana laughing together in the other room, she felt sure that Dana's love would go a long way toward bridging that distance.

And he had once vowed never to have children, afraid he'd be the kind of father their natural father had been. But now his wife was pregnant, and he looked as though he couldn't be happier.

There was hope for him.

"You understand, of course," Anna said, carrying out a tray filled with a pot of her favorite flavored decaf, three cups and a mug of cocoa, "that I'll have to throw you the biggest, most elegant Boston shower known to man."

"What's that?" Will asked.

Anna set the tray on a carved bench she used as a coffee table and sat on the edge of the doe-colored leather sectional where they were all gathered.

"It's a shower that isn't restricted to women. Men can come, too." She poured and distributed cups.

"We just want you to be happy with us," R.J. said, leaning back and sipping his coffee. "You aren't required to do anything else."

"I'm not *required* to do anything at all." Anna scolded him with a look. "But I happen to love both of you, so I'd like to do it for your baby. What's your due date?"

"October seventeenth," Dana replied. "I'm just about nine weeks along." She sighed dreamily and turned to smile at R.J., her eyes alight with love and excitement. "I can't believe we're sitting here, talking about our son—or daughter."

"Can't they tell you what it is?" Will asked.

R.J. shook his head. "We want it to be a surprise."

"But what if you get a lot of pink stuff, and it's a boy?"

Dana laughed. "People usually give you yellow or green when you're not sure."

"Or we'll just save it for the second baby," R.J. said, wrapping his arm around Dana and pulling her toward him to kiss her temple. "God, I'm happy."

"Me, too, darling," Dana mumbled brokenly against his throat. "Me, too."

Will, sitting on the other side of his aunt and uncle, rolled his eyes at their prolonged hug and smiled happily.

Anna nodded, jealousy at work deep down where she hid all private thoughts. But she smiled brightly, forgetting everything else and telling herself she was fortunate to have her son.

When she'd learned she was pregnant with Will, her husband, John, had been unenthused, and for the first month or so her happiness had felt hollow because he hadn't shared it.

Then her family's excitement and her reading and research began to thrill her despite John's lack of interest. The first time she felt the baby move, she realized she already had a relationship with him, and nothing would ever diminish the miracle of that for her.

And nothing ever had. Even when she'd been about to deliver and John had chosen to support a client through a tricky deposition rather than his wife at the birth of their son, she'd approached labor gleefully, eager to see this child she'd come to love so much.

From the moment she first rested her eyes on Will, he'd been everything she'd ever prayed for.

She was delighted that her brother would support his wife throughout her pregnancy. Anna had never regretted a moment of hers, but she imagined it would be wonderful to have a husband's hand to hold through it all. She had never and would never experience that.

"I know it's early," she said as R.J. and Dana drew apart. "But have you thought about names yet?"

"We bought a book that's in the car," Dana said, "But you're commissioned to watch for great names as new clients come through your office."

"How about Austin for a boy?" Will asked eagerly. "Mom's going to do Austin Cahill's wedding to... Mom?"

"Caroline Lamont," she provided.

"I know Cahill." R.J. nodded, as though expressing approval. "Nice guy. Smart. But a cool customer. I met him when I was on the board of Texas Charities, and then I saw him at the gala last month. Nothing gets by him."

"He's buying RoyceCo," Will informed him. "I'd buy some shares, Unc. It's about to go up."

R.J. smiled at his nephew, his expression half affection, half attention. "No kidding. I'll have to look into that. Did you tell Drake?"

Drake Logan was Maitland Maternity's vice president in charge of finance, and he and Will met regularly to talk stocks.

Will shook his head. "I'll tell him when I see him."

"I imagine that'll be quite a wedding," Dana speculated. "I had to call Caroline Lamont when I was soliciting donations for a silent auction your mother was chairing for the Lone Star Ladies, and she sent a litter of wolfhound puppies. They made a bundle on those pups! They'd all had their shots, too, as I recall."

Anna remembered that. "She thinks big. We're doing a medieval English theme complete with armor and horses."

R.J. laughed. "Don't forget to hire someone to follow with a shovel. We'd better move, sis, if we're going to see Mom before she goes to bed."

He stood and pulled Dana to her feet. "Thanks for the coffee, but please don't plan a party. You've got enough to do already."

She hugged him tightly. "It's what I do best,

brother mine. And I'd love to throw a shower for you two. I'm sure I'll have more than enough help from the family. We've all waited a long time to see you married and walking the floors with a teething baby."

He held her away from him and frowned teasingly at her. "That's sadistic."

She smiled shamelessly. "I know. Let us have our little fun."

"So, don't you think Austin's a cool name?" Will asked as R.J. wrapped an arm around him and headed for the door. Anna and Dana followed.

"It is," R.J. agreed. "I like it. We'll put it on the list we're collecting. Of course, Will's a pretty good name, too."

Will grimaced. "It's too ordinary."

"But you, and the grandfather you were named for, have made it special."

They stopped at the door, and Dana patted Will's shoulder. "Names mean different things to different people," she said. "Sometimes you dislike an otherwise beautiful name because you associate it with someone you can't stand. Personally, I think Robert William would be a perfect name for a boy."

"Not Robert," R.J. said.

"But it's your name," Dana insisted.

"You just explained why we hate some names. And I have reason to hate that one."

She sighed wearily. "It's time to put that away."

He opened the door. Though he didn't dispute her statement, something in his stance, in his manner, said he would never forgive his long-missing father. His love for Dana had resolved many things in his life, but not that. Never that.

Anna hugged her sister-in-law. "Congratulations, Dana. I'm so happy for both of you. Start thinking about a list of invitees for the shower because I'm going to begin planning it right away."

Dana kissed her cheek. "Thanks, Anna. I'd love that. *We'd* love that."

As she headed for the car, R.J. lingered an extra moment and asked Anna quietly, "You're okay?"

"Of course," she replied, pretending she had no idea why he asked the question. "Why wouldn't I be?"

"I'm sure it's...hard for you to be happy for us."

She punched his shoulder playfully. "A lot you know. I'm thrilled that the two of you have it all. Go! Dana's waiting for you."

R.J. honked the horn as they backed out of the driveway, and Anna closed the door and looked into her son's concerned expression.

"I should probably learn something about sports," he said as they walked to the sofa.

"Why?" Anna asked in surprise.

"Because if they do have a boy and I'm going to be his older cousin, he'll probably want to learn things from me."

Anna withheld a smile, afraid he'd misunderstand. "I imagine he will."

"And I don't think the stockmarket is going to thrill a little kid."

"Probably not."

"Maybe Uncle R.J. will take me to the gym when

he and Drake and Michael and Uncle Mitchell play basketball.''

"You'll have to ask him.''

They settled onto the sofa again, and Will reclined against his pillows, pulling the throw over him. He continued to look concerned. "You think I'll get killed on the court?'' he asked worriedly. "I'm not very fast. That's why I don't play sports.''

She tried not to make an issue of it. He rode his bike all the time, so she was sure he got enough exercise, but it was a relatively solitary activity, and she often wished he'd get involved in team sports for the social benefits.

"I suppose you could try it. Practice might make you quicker. But if you still don't like it or don't feel comfortable playing, you don't have to. I'm sure your cousin will love you anyway and will have lots of other things to learn from you.''

Will sighed, and she felt his feet resting against her relax.

"My father was really a jerk to not love you,'' he said, turning his face to the television. "You know everything.''

Later, when he was asleep in his bed and she walked through the house turning off lights, checking that the doors were locked, Anna thought maybe she should have recorded that statement to play back to him when he was a teenager and inevitably came to doubt her knowledge and experience.

She felt oddly restless. She was thrilled about her brother's baby, but it would put a little more distance between them, just as his marriage had.

After her divorce, she and R.J. had supported each other in their single lives. She'd accompanied him when he needed a woman on his arm at some function or other, and he'd been her escort when she'd required one. He'd cheerfully gone with Will to father-son functions at school.

But now he had his own family to think of. He had all the things she'd hoped to find with John and failed.

Having glimpsed the possibilities of a marriage based on shared loved made contemplating her single status that much more difficult.

With a toss of her head, she walked upstairs, reminding herself how much she'd hated living with John. The only good thing to come out of their relationship was Will.

She walked into her pink and green bedroom, redecorated last year when she'd been in a mood like the one she was in tonight. Leaning in the doorway, she reflected how perfect it looked, bed linens layered and coordinated, window treatments matching, family pictures hung on the walls and interspersed with beautiful wreaths and swags from Hope Logan's gift shop at the hospital.

She folded her arms and allowed her irrepressible sense of humor to slip into her melancholy mood.

What she needed was an arrangement like Caroline's. She needed some kind, intelligent man to want her simply for sex.

She laughed out loud at that thought. A kind man would never want a woman simply for sex, but she couldn't help but think that it would suit her needs right now.

It was impossible to deny that she was lonely and getting older. There hadn't been time for serious relationships since John had left, and she didn't believe in casual ones. With Will aware of everything, she'd thought it easier to be celibate than to be careful.

But, strangely, that was becoming more difficult as she grew older. She was very aware that soon her chances at finding love would disappear altogether, and it was hard to face the reality that she would never—ever—know what it was like to lie with a man who loved her for herself.

So maybe she should look around for someone who was only interested in sex.

With a sigh, she accepted that she would never do that with Will just down the hall.

She flipped the light off and climbed into her perfect bed, an unbidden image taking shape in her head. It was Caroline Lamont and Austin Cahill standing at the foot of a bed somewhere in Kauai. Long sheer curtains fluttered into the room on the night breeze, revealing a sliver of moon in the sky.

Anna closed her eyes against the picture, annoyed and ashamed that it had come to her. But it persisted.

He was a little cool, she remembered, and he admitted that he was a busy man. Would he take his time? She wondered idly, then hated herself for entertaining the thought. What was wrong with her? She felt like a voyeur.

But she couldn't help it. Then an odd change took place. The naked feminine body in his arms was familiar—hips a little too wide, breasts a little too full. It was her!

While that vision was even more horrifying, it also made it somehow more acceptable to watch as Austin Cahill did everything that she'd dreamed a man would do to her—*for* her.

Her breath grew shallow as the image became real enough for her to feel his touch against her skin, his breath on her cheek, the graze of his knee against her thigh as he rose over her.

With a growl of disgust at herself, she sat up in bed, turned on the bedside light and simply sat there, heart pounding in her chest, fingers trembling.

She experienced a moment of real shock as she realized how deeply she was affected by an adolescent daydream.

Maybe a cold shower would help, she thought half-seriously. She opted instead to go downstairs and give some serious thought to R.J. and Dana's shower.

Planning someone else's party always helped her forget her own deprivations.

CHAPTER THREE

AUSTIN AWOKE to the ringing of the telephone. He squinted sleepily at the travel alarm on the hotel's bedside table as he reached for the receiver. Three-twelve.

His first thought was that something had gone wrong with the deal. But common sense reminded him that it couldn't be that. He'd closed it already.

Then he remembered that his mother was traveling in Africa with her best friends, Dorothy Churchill and Emily Pratt. She'd returned from Ireland the previous year with a knot on her forehead after being lowered by her ankles to kiss the Blarney Stone. What could she have done this time—enraged a rhino or caused an elephant stampede?

"Hello?" he said urgently.

"Hi, Austin! Did I wake you?" It *was* his mother, and the question sounded hopeful rather than apologetic.

"Yes, you did," he answered, relieved at the sound of her voice. "It's just after three here."

"Well, it's ten-fifteen here in Nairobi, and Dot and Emmy and I are having breakfast on our sunporch. Wish you were here."

He propped up on an elbow and laughed lightly.

"Oh, you do not. Having a man along would just cramp your style."

"That's true. The gigolo I'm looking for would think I already had a young man. Are you still getting married?"

He'd stood firmly against her disapproval since he'd announced his plans just before she'd left for Africa. When he'd driven her and her friends to the airport, she'd lectured him on the necessity of marrying for love.

"*You* married for love," he'd told her, "and look at what happened. You held everything together, and if my father hadn't killed himself by driving drunk, you'd still be supporting him."

"It apparently wasn't love on his part, because love gives you comfort and the ability to endure. Austin, I wish you wouldn't think of marriage as just another merger."

"Mom, I'm doing what's right for me."

"You're doing what'll get you a child. That's all."

"A child is all I want."

"That's insane, Austin!"

He'd framed her face in his hands as her flight was called. "Mom," he'd said gently. "You don't exactly set the standard for sanity, so don't judge, all right?"

He'd tried to turn her toward the boarding gate, but she'd taken hold of his lapels and held on, her dark eyes gravely serious.

"Darling, don't do this to yourself," she'd pleaded. "I like Caroline. She's a good friend to you. But don't miss the chance for a love relationship just to have things your way. Please."

Then her friends had tugged on her, and the three of them had disappeared past the gate.

He sat up in the cool bed and said firmly, "Yes, Mom. I'm still getting married."

"You know what'll happen," she predicted. "You'll be married two weeks, and you'll meet someone you'll want to spend the rest of your life with. But it'll be too late."

"That wouldn't happen to me, Mom."

"Austin, everyone is skeptical of love until it happens to them. You think because you saw it fail that it fails all the time. But it doesn't. Dorothy had a wonderful marriage for half a century. Emily was married to Ray for thirty-seven years. And they were happy."

That wasn't precisely the point, but explaining required too much thinking, too much analyzing. And it was three in the morning, for God's sake. "That's great. It's just not for me. You have enough money?"

She emitted a high-pitched sigh, which he recognized as surrender. It was her signal that she was tired of arguing with him.

"You gave me enough money for my birthday to allow me to *buy* Africa. Money isn't everything, you know. I thought I taught you that."

"You did. It's just more reliable than people. Except for you, of course. I love you, Mom. Be careful, okay?"

She made that sound again. "Okay, Austin. But I give you fair warning. When the day comes and the minister asks if anyone has a reason the wedding shouldn't take place, I'm going to speak!"

"Mother…"

"Bye, dear. Dorothy and Emily say hi."

The line went dead, and he cradled the receiver, the room suddenly very dark and very quiet.

Lying back and pulling the covers up, he rested his hands behind his head and listened to the sounds of his loneliness. Quiet, distant traffic, the ticking clock, the nighttime sounds of the hotel—furnace, plumbing, soft steps walking past his door.

He remembered how quiet their Dallas apartment had been at night when he was a child. His father had been out drinking or home sleeping it off. He'd died when Austin was eight, but the house remained quiet because Austin's mother had slept in exhaustion from working twelve hours a day, six days a week just to keep a roof over their heads and food on the table.

Austin could clearly recall lying in bed and worrying about his mother, worrying about himself. He'd loved his father and hadn't understood his need for the booze that rendered him unconscious. And like most children in similar situations, he'd been convinced that something *he'd* done had made his father unable to cope.

He used to wonder if it would drive his mother away one day.

When he felt bold enough to share that worry with her, she'd wept and assured him that nothing in the world would ever separate them until he was old enough to make his own life. He was everything in the world to her, she'd said, and she would always be there for him.

And she had been. She'd slaved with overtime and

extra part-time jobs all through his childhood, until he was old enough to help and finally take over responsibility for their household.

What he'd liked best about money, he thought now, was that generating it created noise and activity. It filled the awful silences where fears bred and worries accumulated.

And so he'd dedicated himself to making money. He had a gift for it and eagerly learned all that he could to turn the gift into a skill.

Was he really missing something, as his mother insisted?

It didn't feel as though he was. He had everything he wanted and, probably within a year, he would have a child. If Caroline chose to stay with him, that would be fine because they were good friends and she was pleasant company.

If she chose to leave, that would be fine, too. Although he liked having her around, he didn't really need her. And he would be there for their baby. He'd learned parenting skills from the very best.

He closed his eyes, relieved to have heard from his mother and to know that she was safe. He was also satisfied with his analysis of his life. He had things perfectly balanced at the moment, and the love his mother was so sure he needed would only unsettle that balance.

Yes. Life was good as it was.

"MOM THINKS this would be the perfect setting for your wedding," Anna said, stopping in the middle of her mother's garden and gesturing around her. "Of course, not all the flowers are in bloom yet, but they should be beautiful in time for your wedding. What do you think?''

She turned to face the couple following her through the garden. The path spilled into a broad expanse of velvety green lawn.

Connor O'Hara and Janelle Davis came toward her hand in hand, he a tall, well-muscled man and she a slender brunette with watchful eyes and an effusive manner. Both looked around appreciatively at the setting.

Their story was one for the soap operas, Anna thought.

Their baby had unwittingly invaded the lives of Anna's mother and her children last September, the day Megan invited the press to Maitland Maternity Clinic to talk about preparations for the hospital's twenty-fifth-anniversary celebration.

The infant lay in a Moses basket on the back step of the hospital, fragile and beautiful, causing a commotion among the hospital staff and the press.

Connor arrived in October, and the Maitland siblings eventually learned that he was their cousin, the adopted son of their father's sister, Clarise.

Janelle came to Austin in January, claiming that she was the baby's mother and Connor his father. She'd explained that she'd abandoned her relationship with Connor because he'd been a workaholic. When she discovered she was pregnant, she'd tried to contact him, only to learn that he'd sold his ranch and moved on.

When she'd given birth to the baby, she had no

job, no money and no family, and she'd heard about Maitland Maternity Clinic.

Anna's mother believed them, but Social Services insisted that Janelle produce the baby's birth records before he could be removed from Megan's foster care. Apparently the records were in New Mexico, and bureaucratic red tape and a fire were interfering with their journey to Texas.

Meanwhile, Megan kept the baby in the hospital's day care while she was at the office, and at home with her at night. Janelle and Connor visited him regularly.

Anna had been suspicious of them at first, but Janelle's sincerity was becoming difficult to question. Anna knew some of her siblings still had doubts, but Megan's happiness at discovering her nephew was all Anna needed to convince her that Connor was genuine.

"This would be perfect!" Janelle said, clutching Connor's arm in her delight. "I can't believe this is happening to us! To think that just seven months ago, I thought I had nothing. I'd given up my man and my baby and I was sure I'd end up spending the rest of my life behind the counter of some fast food restaurant, thinking about what I was missing."

Her voice broke, and Connor drew her closer, smiling apologetically at Anna as Janelle broke down.

She did that a lot, Anna noticed, but then it was an emotional time for all concerned. And it must be killing her not to be able to take her baby home.

"When you make the right decisions," Anna said, "like coming back to claim your baby, things usually turn out well. So let's not waste energy on what you *thought* the future would be when it now includes a newfound family, a wedding to plan and—as soon as the records arrive—the right to take your son home.''

Janelle reached out to pull Anna into her embrace with Connor.

"We're so grateful to you!" she said.

Anna shook her head. "I didn't do anything."

"But you're planning our wedding as a gift!"

Anna shrugged. "You're just lucky enough to have a fiancé whose cousin is in the business. Now, come on. Mom wants us to have coffee with her while we plan the menu for the reception."

ANNA MAITLAND was everything Janelle hated in another human being—in a woman particularly.

She was all grace and good manners and good intentions. And it didn't hurt that she looked like some supermodel who now had better things to do.

It helped soothe Janelle's feelings of hatred and resentment that Anna didn't have a husband. It was nice to know that her privileged life had left her needing something.

And it was also satisfying to know that though she was smart enough to have had that brilliant kid and to own and run her own business, she was still gullible enough to have swallowed the story, hook, line and baby.

She believed that Petey Jones, Janelle's husband, was Connor O'Hara, Megan's long-lost nephew. And she believed that Janelle had really given birth to the little stinker in the house and had turned her life around to reclaim him and give him a loving home.

Ha!

She couldn't wait for the day Miss Grace and Beauty learned the truth.

"HELLO!" Megan Maitland opened the back door, baby in her arms, and called, "Coffee's ready!"

Anna hurried her step. Her mother was the only sixty-two-year-old woman she knew who could run a corporation, know what was going on with every member of her family, happily cope with the daily care of a seven-month-old baby and still look as though she'd never lifted a finger.

She wore a gray-blue wool dress today that lightened her dark blue eyes. Her soft white hair was drawn into her favorite French twist. She had an air of serenity Anna had always wanted to acquire but never quite mastered.

"Hi, Cody," Anna said, reaching out for the baby and settling him on her hip. With her free arm she hugged her mother.

"Chase, Anna," Megan corrected. "Not Cody. You are having a hard time with that."

Anna groaned as she kissed the baby's plump fingers. "Sorry about that. Chase is really a good name for you," she said to the baby, who watched her with big eyes, "because I could just chase you all over then eat you up!" She nibbled at his fingers, and the baby laughed.

When he'd been found on the hospital doorstep, her mother had called him Cody because of the initials C.O. on a baby bracelet he wore. When Janelle came to claim him, she explained that the initials stood for Chase O'Hara.

"I swear, Mom," Anna said, bouncing the baby. "This child must be gaining a pound a day." Janelle and Connor approached, and Anna handed the baby over to his mother.

Megan patted Anna's shoulder. "And we thought that was a quality relegated to Maitland women," she teased.

Anna frowned at her mother. "Not funny, Mom. I did an hour on the treadmill last night." With playful resentment, she turned her frown on Janelle. "You never seem to gain an ounce, Janelle."

The baby reached for Anna with outstretched arms, but Janelle took one of his hands and kissed it and drew him to her. "Now, come on, baby," she said. "Aunt Anna has work to do. You have to sit with me." She disappeared into the house, and Connor followed.

"I swear," Anna said quietly to her mother as they, too, walked into the house, "that baby remembers she left him on your doorstep and refuses to warm up to her."

Megan frowned as she closed the door. "It'll just take time," she said. "He's gotten used to me, and you've helped a lot, so you get the smiles she doesn't get. Poor Janelle. It isn't easy to right that kind of wrong."

"I know." Anna wrapped an arm around her mother's shoulders and walked with her through the sunporch and toward the kitchen. "I'm sure they'll be more comfortable with each other by the time the records prove her parentage."

Megan smiled suddenly, stopping Anna on the threshold to the kitchen. "Isn't it wonderful about R.J. and Dana?"

Anna laughed and hugged her. "Will's so excited. He's going to take up sports so he can teach the baby. I'm planning a Boston shower. You'll have to help me."

"Of course. You're welcome to have it here, if you like."

"That'd be perfect. We can do it in August and have it on the lawn. I still have all those sun umbrellas from that Spalding wedding that never happened. The bride's mother was so upset, she refused to pay for the garden party things her daughter ordered, so I kept them. I have thirty green-and-white-striped umbrellas in my guest bedroom."

"Closed, I hope, or you're in for a lot of bad luck."

"Not me," Anna insisted. "All my bad luck turns to good."

ANNA REMEMBERED what she'd said two hours later when she went to the day-care center at Maitland Maternity to surprise Will by picking him up for lunch. She stopped in confusion when she realized that members of the staff were huddled on the lawn in nervous little groups. Her brother Mitchell stood at the door, shaking his head adamantly as an older man tried to gain entrance.

"Anna!" Hope Logan, who managed the hospital's gift shop, emerged from one of the groups to intercept her as she headed for the entrance. "Anna, you heard! Isn't it awful?"

Dread trickled down Anna's backbone. "Heard what? What's happened?"

"A man's holding the kids in the day-care center hostage!" she exclaimed, her eyes wide with horror. "He thinks Jake's got his wife or something. Or she's run away with him. I didn't get all the…"

Jake was Anna's younger brother, and he had appeared at Christmas with a pregnant woman who still remained a mystery. This wasn't the first time the woman's husband had shown up at the clinic. Anna tore across the lawn, straight for the entrance.

Her brother Mitchell caught her by the shoulders. "You can't go in, Anna. What are you doing here?"

"Will's in there, Mitch!" She tried to shake him off. "There's no school today! And Beth! Let me through."

"Nobody's getting through, Anna." He held her firmly, lowering his voice to reason with her. "Mike and Max are talking to this guy, and the police are on their way. R.J. and Mom were at a meeting, but they're on their way in. I promise you we won't let anything happen to Will, or Beth, or to any of the kids. But we've got to be cool."

Mike was Michael Lord, head of Maitland Maternity's security, and Max was Max Jamieson, a private detective.

Her heart was beating so hard she could hardly form a thought. But she did understand that Mitchell wasn't letting her through.

Mitchell was two years younger than she was, and

the oldest of Megan and William's natural children. So close in age, Anna and Mitchell had fought throughout their childhood, but found a common ground as teenagers and had been good friends ever since. She knew he wouldn't deliberately cause her grief, but at that moment she'd have willingly knocked him unconscious and walked over him to get to her son.

This couldn't be happening, she thought desperately. She'd told Will she was sending him to the day care because she felt more comfortable knowing he'd be looked after.

Now someone was holding him and the other children hostage?

"Mitch," she said, her voice high and tight. "If you don't let me in there, I will not be responsible for what I might do to you."

"Anna, I'm not the one with the gun."

Her heart stalled. "He has a *gun?*"

"Yes," Mitchell said, giving her a small shake. "Now, you don't want to be responsible for making him nervous, do you? I know you're upset, Anna, but the police are coming. And Mike and Max have him talking, and while he's talking, he's not hurting anybody."

"Ms. Maitland."

Austin Cahill appeared beside her, his expression questioning. His eyes went from Mitchell's grip on her arms to her face, which she knew reflected the horror she felt at her son's vulnerability in the hands of a man with a gun.

"Is there a problem?" he asked.

Mitchell explained quickly what had happened. "The best thing to do is wait until the police arrive."

"Mitch," she pleaded. "You don't have children. You don't understa—"

"He's right, Ms. Maitland," Cahill said. "Come on. Let's go wait on the lawn with the others."

"But..."

He took her arm and turned her away from Mitchell, giving her the slightest wink. Another woman ran toward the door, claiming Mitchell's attention.

"We'll try the back door," Cahill said quietly as he walked her around the building.

But one of Mike's uniformed men was there.

"Where is the day care?" Cahill asked, pulling her to the side behind the partial concealment of a hedge.

"Bottom floor," she said, "sort of in the middle, but there's a long corridor off it that goes from a room where the kids hang their coats to the west corner of the building."

"Show me."

"There's only one small window in the coatroom, and it's kind of high up. I don't think I could fit through it."

"Show me where it is."

Anna walked with him around the building, skirting the guard at the back door and rounding the corner to the west side of the hospital, where there was nothing but a narrow, dusty patch of dirt between the building and the property line. Her mother intended to have it landscaped, but had never gotten around to it.

The window was tall and narrow, about six feet off the ground. Anna felt a new clutch of panic as she pointed it out to Cahill. "See how small it is? Well, boost me up anyway and I'll try to..."

Before she could finish the sentence, the bottom pane of glass swung out and upward.

Austin pushed her against the building and got between her and the window.

She watched in horrified fascination as a short pair of jeans-clad legs appeared, first sticking straight out, then dipping and searching with grubby runners for a foothold.

An escape underway?

Austin caught the groping feet, and at the strangled little cry from their owner, who clutched the windowsill for dear life, he tersely whispered, "Sh!"

Catching the legs in one arm, he reached the other up to support a scrawny little chest and brought the child down.

Anna ran to them, recognizing Whitney Westerfield, another ten-year-old who also came to the day care on school in-service days.

"Whitney, are you okay?" she demanded, leaning over the little girl.

Whitney nodded. "Me and Will were in the cloakroom helping the little kids hang up their coats when we came back from the field trip. When we heard the man come in, Will closed the door so he wouldn't know we were there. But it took us a long time to get the window open."

"Is Will okay?" Anna asked, her heart pounding.

Whitney pointed to the window as a small toddler was eased through the opening by a very familiar pair of hands.

"He's going to pass out the little kids to me."

Austin already had the child, and Anna took her from him. She pointed Whitney to the fence and sent the little girl with her. "You stay there with her. How many are there?"

"Six, I think. No, seven."

"Okay, you stay right there!"

The little ones came one after the other as quickly as they could be passed through the window, then were sent to Whitney's post by the fence. The unusual morning's adventure kept the normally chatty two- and three-year-olds quiet.

Anna waited, air trapped in her lungs, for Will to climb out the window. But he didn't come.

"Will!" she whispered harshly.

She turned with a desperate expression to her companion, but he was already taking action.

AUSTIN GRASPED the windowsill and lifted himself until he could see into the dim space. It was hard to tell what was happening. There was yowling and hissing, and a thundering began on the other side of the door.

"Who's in there!" an enraged voice demanded.

Austin turned to the door and saw that the resourceful kid had stacked three little chairs so the one on top prevented the knob from turning all the way. He heard a woman's voice quietly reply, though the words were indistinct.

Before he knew what was happening, two large angry yellow eyes glared at him as a fat gray tabby was thrust to the window. He thanked his years of weight training as he held on to the windowsill with one hand and tried to control the outraged animal with the other.

There was a hiss and the rake of claws down his right shoulder. Then the cat leaped over Austin's back and out the window.

The fist thundered on the door and the knob turned back and forth but remained secure.

Heart in his throat, Austin whispered for the boy to hurry. But the altercation with the cat had caused the stack of boxes and benches he'd propped against the window for height to collapse, and he took precious moments trying to reassemble it.

"Never mind that!" Austin whispered. "Just jump for my hand!"

He saw the boy prepare to comply, then stop suddenly and stare into his eyes. The boy's were wide and brown behind his wire-rimmed glasses, and filled with disbelief.

"Austin Cahill!" he gasped.

Austin remembered Anna Maitland's assertion that he was her son's hero and his refusal to believe it.

The hammering increased in the other room, though it no longer sounded as though it was on the door. It reminded Austin of the urgency of the situation.

"Take my hand!" he ordered. "Now!"

The boy leaped up, and Austin caught a skinny little arm in his hand, praying that he didn't dislocate any bones. He had to drag the boy through the window headfirst, but saw Anna's hands reaching up to catch him.

There were screams on the other side of the door, a crash, then a confusion of voices. It sounded like rescue.

Austin dropped to the ground. Anna Maitland had the boy crushed to her and looked at Austin over the top of his head. In her eyes was the same expression he'd seen in the boy's when he'd stared at him from the cloakroom floor.

It completely unsettled him.

It was adoration.

CHAPTER FOUR

THERE WAS CHAOS at the front of the hospital when Anna, Austin, Will and Whitney came around the building with the toddlers.

Anna's sister Beth, who ran the day care, spotted them and pulled away from the policeman who questioned her to run to Will and wrap him in her arms.

"Are you all right?" she asked, drawing Whitney into her embrace. "When I saw you two close the door to the cloakroom, I didn't know whether to be relieved or more worried!"

"They rescued all the children they had with them." Austin indicated the line of toddlers holding hands between him and Anna. "They were pretty brave and very resourceful."

Beth hugged the two older children again.

"Did they get the guy?" Austin asked gravely.

She shook her head with regret. "When Mike and Max stormed in with the police, he ran through the administration office and out to the parking lot, where he stole a car."

"Will's mom and her boyfriend helped me and Will get the babies out," Whitney said.

Anna raised a startled eyebrow, and Austin turned to her with a look of amusement.

Will's cheeks flamed. "I didn't say he was her boyfriend," he said under his breath to Whitney.

"Yes, you did. You…"

"I said I *wished* he was her boyfriend," he corrected with an apologetic glance at Anna and a mortified look in his hero's direction. "He's marrying somebody else. Mom's just doing his wedding."

Anna struggled against a blush. "Beth, this is Austin Cahill. Mr. Cahill, my sister, Beth Maitland."

"Nice to meet you, Mr. Cahill."

Anna hugged her. Beth, one of the Maitland twins, was tall like their mother, and a free spirit when it came to fashion. She dressed in clothes that were both comfortable and fun, and today wore black capri pants and a baby-blue cropped sweater. Her wavy dark hair fell in loose curls down her back, making her look as vulnerable as a child.

"Are you okay, Beth?" Anna asked. "What a frightening thing for you. Do you have all the children rounded up?"

Beth took command of the toddlers. "This accounts for everybody, thanks to my brilliant nephew." She ruffled Will's hair. "A lot of parents heard the story on the news and came right down, so we're collecting them all in the lobby."

"I think we lost Smokey, though," Will said. "I tried to hand him out the window to Mr. Cahill, but he ran right over his face and down his back."

"He's probably in the bushes somewhere," Beth said. "We'll look for him as soon as everything settles down. Is Will staying, Anna?"

"I was here to take him to lunch." Anna put an

arm around him, wanting to squeeze him to her, but reading the look in his eyes that said, *Please, Mom. Not in front of Austin Cahill and Whitney.* She contented herself with simply knowing he was safe. "I think I'll cancel my afternoon appointments and take him home."

Will rolled his eyes. "Mom. I'm fine. And you have work to do."

Now that the crisis was over, the panic that she had suppressed seemed to be expanding and spreading slowly through her, seeping into her pores, filling her being and her brain with all the things that could have happened.

She felt the need to take him home, where she knew he was safe, and give him cookies and milk and anything else he wanted.

"Why don't I take the two of you to lunch," Austin Cahill suggested, "and then we'll see how you feel." He smiled at Beth. "Is that all right?"

Anna opened her mouth to protest, but Will gave her that look again. *Mom, please,* it said.

Beth nodded. "Of course. Thank you, Mr. Cahill, and you, too, Anna. Would you give me a hand here, Whitney, to get the little ones into the lobby?"

Beth led the parade of children through the crowd, assuming the take-charge authority that made her day care so successful.

"Where's your favorite place to go for lunch?" Cahill asked Anna.

Now that her pulse was settling down, Anna wondered why he'd been at the hospital this morning.

"What were you doing here, Mr. Cahill?" she asked, ignoring his question.

He pointed to the bank on the corner. "Bank machine. I have every credit card know to man, but I'm always out of cash. I saw the commotion and came to see what was going on." That explained, he turned his attention to her son. "Where would you like to have lunch, Will?"

Will was speechless. He opened his mouth to reply, but nothing came out.

"Mr. Cahill," Anna said, thinking that maybe an introduction would help, "this is my son, Will. Will, Mr. Cahill."

Cahill reached a hand out to him. "I'm pleased to meet you, Will," he said, swallowing her son's much smaller hand in his large one. "I'm very impressed with your quick thinking."

Will flushed purple again, and though he shook hands, he still seemed unable to speak.

"Your mom tells me you're interested in business."

Will managed a nod.

"And that you read *Forbes* and take care of her stock portfolio."

"Yes." Will's voice came out high and squeaky, but he cleared his throat and tried again. "Yes. And my aunts'. My uncle R.J. helps me, and Drake Logan."

"Drake is Maitland Maternity's vice president in charge of finance," Anna explained.

"I know R.J. Maitland," Austin said, walking them

toward the parking lot. "We served on a committee or a board together, I think."

Will, who never forgot anything, said, "Texas Charities. He told Mom he knew you. He said you were a smart man."

Cahill laughed. "I try to be well informed. That can be better than being smart. Here we are."

He stopped beside a sporty red Mercedes and opened the passenger door, then pushed the front seat down so Will could climb into the back.

But Anna caught her son's arm to stop him.

"Mr. Cahill, this really isn't necessary," she insisted. "And Caroline…"

"Caroline and her bridesmaids are shoe shopping in Dallas today." He looked into her eyes as though trying to read her thoughts. "She's not the jealous type, if that's what you're worried about. I just thought that we're all a little rattled and it would be good to celebrate Will's quick thinking."

Of course. That was a simple and logical explanation. It wasn't that she didn't want to go with him, because she did—very much.

More than she should.

"Mom," Will complained. "You're pinching my arm."

She let him go, deciding that if she did this for her son rather than for herself, it would be all right.

He scrambled into the back seat. Cahill saw her into the front, closed her door, then walked around the hood and climbed in behind the wheel.

"Where do we want to go?" he asked, looking into the rearview mirror at Will.

"Let's have steak!" Will replied, leaning forward over the seats. "All Mom ever wants for lunch is salad."

Will, Anna thought, was recovering from his shyness with a vengeance.

"Something simple," she began, "would be—"

"My hotel," Cahill interrupted, "has a great dining room with everything you can think of on the menu. You can have your salad and Will can have his steak."

He was staying at the Austin Palace, she knew, the most exclusive hotel outside Dallas, and while she and her family often went there, she didn't want Cahill to think she was taking advantage of his simple offer of lunch.

But he was already out of the parking lot and heading in that direction, so it seemed futile to argue.

The King's Room was a sea of crisp white linen, gleaming, gold-rimmed china and sparkling silverware. Bluebonnets sat in a crystal vase on each table, and an army of waiters stood by to answer every need.

Austin was greeted with a deference that suggested he was divine. Then Anna realized that when he'd referred to the dining room and said in *my hotel,* he'd meant that in the most literal sense. He wasn't simply staying there. He owned it.

THE BOY WAS LIKE the beam of a flashlight in the dark, Austin thought. He was bright enough to be blinding.

"What you did with that hotel chain in the mid-Atlantic states was amazing," Will said, his eyes wide with excitement, all his earlier shyness evaporated. "Day cares in every hotel is being done all over, but hot tubs and computer centers in every room is a great idea. A lot of businessmen carry laptops, but now they can scan things or send faxes...."

It was very odd to listen to insightful observations about business coming out of the mouth of a child under five feet tall. Austin tried not to reflect his amusement—and amazement—in his response.

"We're hoping it'll triple occupancy."

"Drake thinks that if the hotels are well run, you'll have full houses all year long in that part of the country. He calls it the commercial flyway. You know, like birds in the Atlantic flyway? Except that it's businessmen going back and forth all the time."

"That's about right. Of course, a lot of business goes on right here in Texas."

"I know," the boy replied. "We have eight hundred and twenty-five high-tech companies in Austin alone."

"I didn't know that."

"I looked it up for a report on computers."

Will's soft drink arrived along with Austin's coffee and Anna's iced tea.

While the boy took a moment away from their discussion to consume half his drink, Austin turned to Anna to compliment her on her son, and found her watching him with pride.

Where Will was like a flashlight, she was like a candle—a soft, quiet light that brightened gently.

He remembered her desperation to get to her son, her silent help in moving the children, the tortured expression on her face when they'd heard pounding on the cloakroom door while Will was still inside.

He could tell by Will's appearance that he was well cared for, and by his easy conversation and his enthusiasm that he was listened to and taken seriously. And not simply because he was a little business genius, but because he was everything to her.

God. He hoped he and Caroline would have a boy. And how he hoped he'd turn out like Will.

"I think I've found an armorer," Anna said. She pulled off the gray jacket of her suit, exposing the light blue sweater underneath. The soft color gave her roses to her cheeks.

He pushed his chair back to take the jacket from her, but she gestured for him to remain seated.

"I'll just put it on the back of my chair." As she turned, her bosom was beautifully outlined in the sweater.

His eyes lingered there for a moment while she adjusted the jacket and Will concentrated on his drink.

Then he realized she'd asked him something, but his brain seemed to have stopped processing information.

"I think having armor at your wedding is so cool!" Will said, putting his fingertip to the top of his straw and raising it out of the glass to watch the cola stream back into it. "Are you going to get to wear some?"

Anna frowned her disapproval at his little game. He dropped the straw into the glass and pushed it away.

Armor. Right. The wedding. "Uh...no, I don't

think so," Austin replied. "I think it's for the ushers waiting outside the church to welcome everyone."

"But you're going to ride in on a horse!"

Austin hoped Anna would dispute that. "Am I?"

She smiled sympathetically. "I think that's the plan."

"Does he wear a crown?" Will wanted to know.

"I'm not sure." Anna replied.

Austin didn't remember Caroline mentioning that, but *he* was sure. "I am *not* wearing a crown."

Her smile was a little more amused than sympathetic. "I believe Caroline's wearing a coronet of flowers."

"I'm also not wearing a coronet of flowers," he assured her.

"You do ride a horse, though?"

He sighed and leaned back in his chair. He did have horses on his ranch outside San Antonio, but he didn't get there nearly as often as he wanted to.

"I do," he answered. "I have a couple of cow ponies on my ranch, some thoroughbreds."

Anna blinked at him. "Then...*you* could provide the horses for the wedding."

"Sure. Unless she's insisting we use Belgians, or whatever the knights rode."

Anna laughed. "I think we can bend authenticity here. I believe Caroline's planning on six. And she said she'd like them all to be the same color."

"I have eight bays."

"Perfect!"

"Horses wore armor, too, you know," Will informed them.

"Well, let's not tell Caroline," Austin said.

Anna shook her head. "Too late. She knows. I'm to look into it. She's done her research."

Austin groaned.

Their lunch arrived—steaks for Will and Austin, an oriental chicken salad for Anna—and some time was spent passing condiments back and forth, rolls and butter, and sugar for Austin's coffee. When Anna found the artificial sweetener cup empty, Austin called for the waiter.

The small, slender man was abjectly apologetic.

"It's all right, Albert," Austin said kindly, as though surprised by his manner. "It happens. Just fill it up, please. The lady needs some for her tea."

"Yes, sir." Albert ran off with the container. A man in a black suit waited for him at the door of the kitchen, his arms folded and a deep frown on his face. Anna guessed he was the restaurant's manager.

"Oh, no." She pointed her fork toward the kitchen. "I hope I didn't get Albert in trouble. He looks nervous."

Austin looked over his shoulder just in time to see Jekel, the restaurant manager, hold the door for Albert and grumble at him as he passed through. He thought he'd noticed a particularly serious note to the wait staff's behavior. Formality in fine dining was appreciated, but the unwillingness—or inability—to smile was not.

He'd have to watch that and try to determine if they were straining to make a good impression on him, or if the oppressive atmosphere pervaded the restaurant.

"Don't worry," Austin said. "I'm his boss, remember?"

"You just took over RoyceCo," Will said, half his steak already gone. "They've needed help for a long time. May I have the steak sauce, please?"

"Yes, they have." Austin passed it. "Grain's a new thing for me, but I thought I'd see how it goes."

"What are you going to do about the puppies?"

Austin couldn't believe this kid. "How did you know about the pet shops? That wasn't in *Forbes*."

"It was in the *Wall Street Journal*." Will carefully poured sauce then capped the bottle and handed it back. "Right under an article about how they've been in violation of animal protection laws for years," he said. Then he smiled hopefully. "That's why you bought RoyceCo, isn't it? To take care of the dogs."

Austin felt the emotional tug of the boy's earnest dark eyes. For a moment it confused him, disoriented him.

This was hero worship in its purest form. The boy knew everything about his business career, yet he was convinced Austin had purchased a major grain company to make a better world for the animals in their subsidiary pet shops.

His eyes swung to the boy's mother, and something he saw there upset him further. Just an hour ago, she'd looked at him with adoration because he'd saved her son. But now she knew—or suspected— that he was more practical and ruthless in his business dealings, and her look had become a little disdainful. Just as it had yesterday when she and Caroline had talked about the reason for the wedding.

Well, she was right, he told himself. This little interlude with them had been a sweet escape from the nothing-for-nothing world he lived in, but that was all it was. Ninety minutes out of a very strange and dramatic day that had made him do things he didn't normally do.

He had to set the boy straight.

"No," he replied quietly. "I'm going to sell the pet shops. I bought RoyceCo for the grain. The pet shops aren't really worth very much."

Will stared at him in silence for a moment, as though he'd misunderstood. "But...they're just puppies."

Austin nodded. "Someone will take care of them," he insisted. "Pet shops are a hassle because the government's watching you all the time and business is tough enough without that added pressure."

Will's face fell. "The last time the inspector went through the one in Dallas, half the puppies were sick."

"Pet care is time-consuming and tricky," Austin said. "I don't have time for that."

"But, you could hire somebody."

"It'll be easier to sell off the pet shops."

"What if somebody buys them who's no better than RoyceCo was?"

"Will, that's enough," Anna said, pointing to his plate. "Mr. Cahill didn't bring us to lunch for you to interrogate him. I'm sure he knows the best way to conduct his business, whether or not we agree with it."

"We?" Austin asked.

She looked him in the eye. She was now not so much a candle in the dark as a torch. "I think Will's right. Puppies are sick. That has to be somebody's responsibility."

"Ms. Maitland..."

"If we're going to quarrel," she said with dark humor, "you may call me Anna."

And the day grew even more strange.

"Anna." He put down his knife and fork. "Companies buy other companies all the time. You keep what's profitable and most practical to deal with, and you sell off what you don't want to someone for whom that aspect of the company *is* profitable and practical. It's business."

"We're accountable for every moment of our lives," she said, "whether conducted in a business setting or anywhere else. And when the day comes that we're asked to explain our actions, I don't think telling Saint Peter that 'It's business' is going to send your elevator up instead of down."

Will looked in mystification from his mother to Austin. "What?" he asked.

Austin smiled at him. "I think your mother just told me I'm going to hell."

"Mom!" Will gasped.

"Finish your lunch, Will," she said, and ignored both of them to finish hers.

Austin drove them to Maitland Maternity's parking lot.

Anna thanked him courteously for lunch and, towing Will behind her, headed for the front doors.

"Thanks!" Will shouted to Austin as his mother dragged him away. "Bye! Think about the puppies!"

ANNA SAW WILL into the day-care center, where order had been restored. Several parents lingered, more for their own reassurance than their offspring's. The children had settled back into their usual routines, seemingly unconcerned about the morning's excitement.

Anna overheard one of the parents saying that Vincent Eckart was responsible for the morning's events. This was at least the second time he'd come to the clinic in search of his estranged wife, Camilla, and Anna's youngest brother, Jake. Anna wondered why Eckart had thought that holding a group of children hostage would help him find his wife.

Ty Redstone, Beth's fiancé and a police detective, also lingered, a child on his hip, as though he couldn't quite bring himself to leave Beth. Anna was helping plan their wedding with traditional Native American pipe-and-drum music, storytelling and Crow garb.

He waved at Anna from across the room, and she blew him a kiss, happy that her sister had found such a wonderful man—and that she'd survived to wear the strapless sheath draped with lace they'd picked out together.

She was also happy to see that Smokey the cat was fast asleep in his customary spot on the television despite the morning's adventure. She and Will went to pet him.

Some of the children were reading, some were coloring, some danced in a circle wearing silly hats, Beth leading them. She waved at Anna and Will.

"You sure you'll be okay?" Anna asked Will, feeling clingy and reluctant to leave him.

"Will!" A little red-haired boy about four ran up to Will and hugged his waist. "Are you gonna read me the dinosaur book now?"

Will patted the redhead in a very adult gesture of affection. "Yeah, Justin. I just have to say bye to my mom. You go get the book and that big blue pillow."

Justin ran off, and Will walked Anna to the door. "I'll be fine, Mom. Don't worry. You're going to come for me when you're done?"

"Right. You want me to ask Rojalia to make something light for dinner since you had that steak? I think she was planning chicken fajitas and salad."

"Yum!" he said. "I love that."

"Okay, then. See you later. Love you."

"Love you, too."

Anna walked to her car, replaying in her mind her conversation with Austin Cahill and wondering if Will was right and she had been harsh in her opinion. He had possibly saved her child's life, after all. And he was her client, though he might have changed his mind about that by now.

She was completely surprised when she almost collided with Austin Cahill a moment later. He leaned against the door of her car, obviously waiting for her.

"Anna," he said with a smile.

"Mr. Cahill," she began, not sure if she intended an apology or more condemnation.

But he interrupted her. "If you're going to consign me to hell, you can call me Austin."

She tried not to smile. "What is it?" she asked. "Did you forget something?"

He straightened from the car and faced her, hands in the pockets of his dark suit. "No, I just wanted to tell you what a clever little genius your son is. I presume he gets all that from you?"

She relaxed a little, loving to talk about Will. "I like to think that a lot of his good qualities and his intelligence come from my side of the family—although it's not the Maitland family you know."

He raised an eyebrow in question.

"My brother R.J. and I were born to William Maitland's brother, Robert, and his wife. But our mother died when I was just a few months old, and our father left us in William's care. Fortunately Megan, his wife and now my mother, was openhearted enough to welcome us and love us like her own."

Austin nodded. "My own father was an alcoholic and hardly knew my mother and I were there. It's hard to believe there are people who can so completely disregard their responsibilities."

She detected the slightest note of bitterness in his voice. He sounded like R.J.—as though he'd learned to deal with the past but couldn't quite move on.

"I guess that's true," she agreed. "But I remember none of that so I'm not much affected by it. All I can recall is a wonderful childhood in the bosom of a warm and loving family."

He nodded and smiled. "That should be every child's reality."

"Yes." She dug into her purse for her keys. "It should. Unfortunately, the world is full of men who can walk away—or look away—from their families without a second thought."

She was a little surprised she'd said that. She usually didn't discuss John or make reference to him with anyone outside her family.

Austin was watching her and, apparently, reading her mind. "We're talking about Will's father?"

She beeped the door open. "But *I* left *him*, so I guess he shouldn't bear all the blame."

"Another alcoholic?"

"Philanderer. Eventually even with a client in our bed."

A pleat appeared between his eyebrows. "A man like that deserves only contempt."

"He does, because Will was only two at the time, and since then, he's seen his father maybe twice, when he came home for his parents' funerals. That's the reason Will has my family's surname."

"I'm sorry. I suppose Will's probably better off without his influence, but I know he'll always wonder what he did wrong. And his father's missing the development of an amazing child."

"That's what selfishness gets you," she said, reaching for her door. But a large hand slid past hers and opened it for her.

He held the door open, but blocked her entrance with a hand on top of the window. "You think I'm selfish," he said, "because all I want out of marriage is a child."

A hearty affirmative was on the tip of her tongue,

but she held it back. Now that she'd seen him in action, scooping children out of harm's way, she couldn't help but feel a certain sympathy toward him.

In fact, what she felt was stronger than sympathy, but it was all too complicated to explore.

"I think you're...unrealistic," she said diplomatically. "You expect to make love to a woman with sufficient...enthusiasm to produce an heir, remain with her for nine months while this baby develops inside her and you listen to its heartbeat and feel it kick, hold her hand while she endures a grueling eternity of labor, and think that once this baby is born you'll simply be able to say goodbye to her? Or that she'll be able to leave that little person who's been part of her body all that time and just disappear?"

"She can stay if she wants to," he said.

"As what? A disinterested third party?" She closed her eyes and summoned patience. "Austin, usually love breeds life. That's how families are born. But life also breeds love. You won't be able to watch the miracle unfold over nine months and not get involved with Caroline."

"Yes, I will," he insisted. "I'm never involved. I have friends, but I don't have lovers in the real sense of the word."

She had to ask. "Are they unable to reach *you*, or are you unwilling to allow *them* access?"

He shrugged, as though the failing within himself was something he'd accepted. "I don't know. I love my mom and I love my friends, but I'm incapable of sharing my life. It's hackneyed but true. If you let people inside, they can hurt you."

"It's impossible to live and never be hurt."

"It's not going to happen to me a second time."

She shook her head. "Then how do you expect to cope with a child? Do you expect this baby to deal with a man who has a stockade fence around him?"

"All a child needs is the man in me." His smile was roguish and prideful. "I have that in abundance. I will care for and protect my child with everything I have."

"Because the child's a part of you," she asked coolly, "or because you want to leave your financial empire to someone?"

"Both."

"What if Caroline doesn't want to leave? What if she wants to mother this baby?"

He shook his head. "I know her. She won't. That's why I chose her."

He seemed so sure of himself. She'd love to be around when Caroline had his baby and everything he expected collapsed under the weight of real life.

"Be prepared," she warned, taking his sturdy wrist and removing it from her car door, "for the woman who delivers your baby to be very different from the woman you made love to. Motherhood changes you. You'll take a lamb on your honeymoon and watch a lioness give birth to your baby."

He held the door while she slipped into her seat and brought her knees up to tuck them under the wheel.

"That may have happened to you," he said, looking at her. "But it won't happen to her."

"Why not?" she challenged.

He leaned down and said quietly, "Because she'd put butterflies in boxes." Then he straightened, closed her door and waved as he walked to his car.

CHAPTER FIVE

"OKAY, I'll come to lunch," Connor said to Megan and Anna the following week as they flanked him, arms tucked into his. They walked him up the street from the hospital to Austin Eats. "But I don't understand why we're doing this."

Megan shook her head. "You have to belong to this family," she said wryly. "There are moments when you're really slow. I told you about Sara at the restaurant. The young woman who has amnesia."

"Right," he said. "I've seen her when I've gone in there. But I told you, I don't know anyone named Sara."

"I know." Megan agreed, "but you said yourself you haven't been in the diner for some time now, and a few weeks ago Sara spoke the name Connor completely out of the blue."

"But I'm not the only Connor in the world," he protested under his breath as they walked into the restaurant.

Megan patted his arm patiently. "But you're the only one we have handy. Just be a love and do this for me."

"Okay," he said grudgingly, letting Megan slip into the corner booth, then sitting beside her. "But just for you. Not because I believe this is going to serve any purpose.''

Anna reached across the table to pat his hand. "Relax, Connor. We're all conditioned to humoring Mom. And now that she's getting older and more eccentric, we're forced to do it more often."

Megan sent her a punitive glare, then focused her attention when Shelby Lord, the diner's owner, started toward them, a bright smile on her face. Megan quickly explained why they wanted to see Sara, and Shelby slipped into the kitchen to locate her.

"Hello," Sara said, appearing a few minutes later. "Shelby told me you wanted to see me."

"Sara," Megan began, "you've met my nephew, Connor O'Hara. We heard about you speaking the name suddenly, and hoped maybe..."

"Connor." Sara studied his face thoughtfully, a furrow appearing on her forehead, then turned back to Megan. "I'm sorry, Mrs. Maitland, but I don't recognize your nephew except from the diner. Each day I'm remembering more things I can do and things I knew, but not people. Or faces." She sighed. "But I'm trying to be patient. I'm sure it's coming." She smiled from Anna to Connor. "I'll send a waitress over now so you can order. Enjoy your lunch."

Megan looked disheartened when Sara went back to the kitchen. "Well, that was disappointing."

"I told you I didn't know her, Aunt Megan," Connor said.

"Well, I thought seeing you might stimulate her memory—if there was a connection with the name."

"Why is it so important to you?"

"Because I'm fond of Sara," Megan replied with a disappointed glance at Anna. "I'd have been pleased if she did have some link with us."

Anna reached across the table to take her mother's hand. She'd always admired the way her mother took responsibility for everything and everyone. She never hesitated to help if she could.

"She does have a connection to us," Anna said. "She's a friend. It's all right that you can't solve her problems, Mom. She'll be fine."

Once they'd placed their orders, they chatted for a while about the upcoming weddings in the family. Connor's interest was halfhearted, and when Anna turned to him to include him in the conversation, she was startled by a dark, almost malevolent expression on his face as he stared across the restaurant.

She followed the line of his gaze and saw Sara standing in the open kitchen window, garnishing the plates on the counter.

Connor turned to Anna, the expression still in place.

Her heart thudded, and a little ripple of unease shivered along her spine.

Then he smiled, and the look was wiped away, his usual affability in his eyes. "Can you imagine the trouble I'd be in with Janelle if I *did* know Sara?"

Megan laughed, and she and Connor exchanged a little light banter on the subject of flattering jealousy, but Anna tuned it out. She was too unsettled by that glimpse inside the man she'd come to believe was her cousin.

Why would anyone look at pretty little Sara like

that—as though she'd done him some irreparable harm and he was plotting dark revenge?

Anna was so startled and confused that the rest of lunch was a chore. What troubled her most was the belief that Connor had lied about knowing Sara before. How could he feel hatred for someone he'd barely met?

She watched him while he talked and joked with her mother, and by the time lunch was over she wondered if she'd imagined that dark look.

But she knew she hadn't, because she still felt oddly unsettled—even frightened.

Connor left them in front of the restaurant to meet Janelle. "We're going to a travel agent to see about a honeymoon cruise," he said. "I'd prefer to go backpacking, but Janelle's into being pampered and lazy."

Megan nodded. "That would be my idea of a vacation. Have fun, and thanks for indulging your aunt."

He leaned down to kiss her cheek. "Anytime." Then he hugged Anna. "Bye."

She forced a smile. "Bye, Connor."

He looked into her eyes, and she did her best to hide her concern, but his eyes lingered on her an extra moment and she wondered if he'd detected something.

Finally he left with a cheerful wave and loped toward the hospital parking lot where he'd left his car.

Anna stared after him worriedly. "You're sure about him, Mom?" she asked.

Megan looped her arm in Anna's. "Sure about what?"

"That Connor's who he says he is."

"I am," Megan assured her, heading down the street. "Why? I thought you were as convinced as I am."

"I was. But…I don't know…I just saw an expression on his face that worries me."

"What do you mean? You know he didn't want to do this in the first place."

"I know. I think he might know Sara, after all."

"But Sara didn't know him."

"Well, she wouldn't, would she? Unless her mind's willing to let her remember—which it doesn't seem to be."

Megan stopped in the middle of the sidewalk and frowned at Anna. "But why would he lie about that?"

Anna shrugged. "I've no idea. But I saw him watching her and he looked…threatening."

"Threatening?" Megan echoed in disbelief.

"Threatening," Anna repeated. "I know it sounds crazy. He's always so kind and friendly, but he looked anything but when he was focused on her."

Megan started walking again, drawing her along. "Anna, you must have imagined that—or misread what you saw. He loves the baby and seems to have endless patience with Janelle—who is a dear but tries *my* patience sometimes. I can't imagine him threatening anyone and I've spent more time with him than you have."

Anna knew that was true, but she also knew what she'd seen.

"I just think you should keep your guard up, Mom," she said.

Megan clutched her arm a little tighter and smiled fondly. "The trouble with you Anna, is that you're everybody's big sister, sometimes even mine. You have the need to take care of everyone. Well, I'm not senile yet, you know, and no one pulls the wool over my eyes. So quit worrying."

"Okay, okay," Anna replied, but she made a mental note to alert R.J., Mitchell and Jake. "I wasn't suggesting you were senile, just that you're very precious to all of us and I'd hate to see anyone hurt you—physically or emotionally."

"Well, that's very sweet, dear."

Anna suddenly realized they'd walked three blocks toward town. "Where are we going, anyway?"

"I have to buy Connor and Janelle a wedding present. I thought you could help me."

"Sure. What did you have in mind?"

Megan stopped in front of the fluttering banners of an automobile agency. "A car," she replied.

JANELLE AND PETEY walked side by side past a block of little boutiques.

"God, it feels good to be away from them!" Janelle exclaimed, ripping out the clip that confined her dark mane and shaking her head. "I spent all morning with Abby, Beth and Ellie shopping for bridesmaids' dresses for Beth's wedding, and I swear I'm within a breath of screaming bloody murder!"

Petey stopped to study the golf clubs in the window

of a sporting goods shop. "Sucking up to rich folks isn't as easy as you thought?"

She groaned and held her hair clip in front of his face, her index finger pinched in its teeth. "That's just how I feel, as though I'm being squeezed in one of those rooms with spiked walls like you see in fantasy movies. Those girls are so *sweet* and so *polite!* How can women be like that and survive?"

"Money," he replied, walking on. "Money's the answer to everything. And I can't wait until we get ours."

"I know. But we have to bide our time to make sure we get as much as we can. Your 'mother' is just giving us stuff right and left."

"Yeah, well, I've got a little surprise for you. I had a lunch date with Megan today."

She rolled her eyes impatiently. "I know that."

"She and Anna and I went to Austin Eats next to the hospital. And you know why we went there?"

Janelle paled. "Petey, I told you to stay away from the diner. You can't have any association with Lacy Clark."

Petey grabbed her arm and squeezed until she gasped and fell silent. "It wasn't my idea, you little witch—Megan took me there to see if I was the Connor sweet little Sara mentioned out of the blue."

Janelle shook her head. Why had they waited so long to get rid of Miss Goody Two-shoes? Was Lacy really starting to get her memory back? That could mean the end of everything! All the months of planning, of waiting for the right moment, of putting up with these damnably sugary people—one word from Lacy and it could all be lost! Lost!

She tried to quell the panic and think. It was always easier just to blame Petey.

"You were supposed to have killed her by now." She lashed out at him. "If you weren't such a coward—" When Petey raised his arm, she took a step back. "Don't you dare touch me. You were supposed to have done the job months ago. Now we're in a real mess, and I'm going to have to get us out of it—yet again."

"We'll have to be careful," Petey warned.

She turned to him impatiently. "Really. I thought we'd just stand her up in the middle of the hospital parking lot and run her over with a truck. At noon, when everyone's going to lunch and can watch us!"

He studied her for a moment with an expression of disbelief, then realized she was joking and burst into laughter.

Janelle rolled her eyes. He might be good-looking, but when it came to brains… How had she ever ended up with the lunk?

HAL GORDON, the armorer Anna found in the town of Elgin, was clearly confused by her request.

He had thick gray hair, though she guessed he was not yet forty, biceps the size of footballs and a welding mask tipped up on his head so he looked a little as though he wore armor himself. Will would have wandered into the room to explore, but Anna held him back.

"You want armor for a wedding?" he asked.

Anna nodded.

He grinned. "Wouldn't it be easier for the couple to get counseling?"

She appreciated his sense of humor. "They're not going to joust in it. Their wedding has a medieval theme and they want their ushers to stand in front of the church properly dressed."

"Ah. Well. Please come in and I'll show you what I have already made. When's the wedding?"

"August."

"Mmm. That's enough time to start from scratch. But first I can show you what I have."

Two men were working in a far corner of the warehouse-like studio, one holding a metal plate in a fire pit, the other pounding a piece of metal on a large table made of half timbers. The sound was almost musical in its repetition.

Gordon took them to an area by the windows where breastplates and backpieces hung from a wire like a very eccentric string of laundry. Some breastplates, she noted, were beautifully etched with designs of figures, flowers or gold scrolled stripes. She stared in astonishment at the artistic workmanship.

"These are English," Gordon said.

"Wow!" Will was as fascinated as she.

They passed a table covered with weapons of the period—swords, broadaxes, a mace, a dagger, a halberd. Beside them were several shields—a very simple round one and several of the more heraldic shape familiar from paintings and illustrations.

"Wow!" Will said again, his voice a little higher.

He stopped to study the objects on the table with fascination.

Anna smiled at her host. "It doesn't seem to matter how much a mother preaches peace, boys are fascinated by weapons."

Hal Gordon laughed. "I know. I was the same way. I think it's some primal memory of long ago when a good weapon was all that stood between you and extinction." He pointed toward the table. "Of course, nowadays you'd have to be very determined to use any of these—they're very heavy, and you have to get up close and know what you're doing."

Anna gave Will a gentle shove along the line of suspended armor. "I think it would be rude to bring weapons to a wedding."

Gordon led the way down the string until they reached several pieces that appeared to be pleated.

"These are German," he explained. "Part of a pucker suit. It copies the pleated clothing of the period."

"I like that one!" Will said

Anna nodded. "It's wonderful, isn't it? But our theme is English, so we'd better stick to something appropriate. Mr. Gordon, do you have four full suits of armor?"

He smiled broadly. "I do. One is for a man five feet ten or so. The other three would accommodate a man six feet tall. If these work for you, I can give you a deal. These pieces have been around for a while."

Anna guessed it wasn't every day that he could make such a sale.

"Good. I should return with my client and make sure she has ushers to fit the suits."

He reached into the pocket of his leather apron and handed her a business card. "Call me anytime."

"Mom, look!" Will caught her arm and pulled her toward a stack of old crates. Arranged artistically atop the one uppermost was the piece of armor that fit atop a horse's head.

"That's a shaffron," Gordon said, touching the part fitted with openings for the ears and eyes and extending to protect the muzzle. "This part—" he ran a hand lovingly over the jointed piece that protected the neck "—is called the crinet. It flexes on sliding rivets and internal leathers." He demonstrated for them.

"That's just what she wanted!" Will said, then added with a smile of delight, "Mom, this place is so cool. Can we just look around for a little while?"

"I imagine Mr. Gordon is pretty busy," she replied.

Gordon shook his head. "I'd love to show him around. Would you like to join us?"

Anna glanced at her watch. "Thank you, but I should make a call. Is there a phone I could use?"

He ushered her to a small and comfortably messy office, then took Will to watch the man at the forge.

Anna dialed Caroline Lamont, wanting to quote her the price for four suits of armor before troubling her to travel thirty miles to look at them. As she waited for Caroline to pick up, she heard the subtle change of ring that indicated the call was being transferred, probably to her cell phone.

She was surprised and momentarily speechless when Austin Cahill answered with a terse, "Cahill."

When she took a moment to reply, he asked, "Hello?"

"Mr. Cahill," she said finally, mustering all the dignity of the woman in charge she presented to her nervous brides. No one had to know it was put on for their benefit. "It's Anna Maitland."

There was the briefest pause, then he said, "I thought we'd decided to be Austin and Anna."

She did like the sound of that. But it wasn't safe, and it definitely wasn't sane. "That was only if we were quarreling or if I was consigning you to hell. Is Caroline there?"

"I'm afraid she's gone to Galveston to replace her sister in a charity fashion show. Camille has the flu. She'll be gone a couple of days. Fittings, all that stuff."

"Oh." Even Anna heard that small sound reflect her disappointment.

"Is there anything I can do?" he asked, then added dryly, "Provided it doesn't involve colors, flowers or fabrics."

"It involves the armor," she said. "I've found an armorer who does the most exquisite work you've ever seen, but it's obscenely expensive. He can give us a deal on armor he's already made, but there's also the question of whether or not they'll fit the men for whom they're intended." She gave him the dimensions Gordon had specified. "I thought you and Caroline should know that before I arrange for you to see it."

"We know she wants armor. And I think they'd fit our ushers."

"Yes, but it's—" She reeled off the cost of four full suits.

"I gave her an unlimited budget."

She couldn't help an exasperated gasp. "I *know,* but that'd pay a semester of your child's tuition at Yale, or buy a very nice car, or—"

"Where are you?" he interrupted.

"Gordon Armory in Elgin."

"Will it upset your schedule for the rest of the day if you wait for me to meet you there?"

It might upset *her,* but not her schedule. "Uh…no. Since it's Saturday, I have Will with me. This was all I had scheduled today."

"All right. I'll be there as quickly as I can."

Will, trying to heft a mace and unable to get it off the ground, grunted with approval when she told him they'd wait for Austin Cahill.

"I'll bet he could…ugh!…lift this!"

He could lift it, she discovered an hour later. He could even swing it over his head.

And now that Hal Gordon had a fitting opponent willing to work—or play—with his creations, he became less a man trying to make a sale than an artist delighted to show off his work.

The serious business of fulfilling Caroline's wishes for her fanciful wedding was pushed aside as the men prepared to stage combat in the empty space in the middle of the warehouse.

"If he hits you with that," Anna argued, indicating

the broadsword Gordon had given Austin for the duel, "he'll slice your arm off!"

Austin smiled at her as he slipped his arm into the leather straps that held the shield in place. Gordon had outfitted Austin and himself with a breastplate and backpiece. "The edge is blunted. And he won't hit me."

"Even blunted, it's heavy enough to crush bone."

He focused on her, some turbulence deep in his eyes working its way to their bright surface, the smile still in place. "You're worried about me," he observed softly.

Somehow she was reminded of the robot in the old television series *Lost in Space* flailing his arms and shouting, "Danger, Will Robinson!" Only this time, he was shouting, "Danger, Anna Maitland!"

She angled her chin to deflect any suggestion that he was anything to her but a client. "You haven't given me your deposit yet," she said.

He held her gaze for a moment, and she couldn't determine whether or not he believed her. Then he turned to Will.

"William," he said.

Will straightened at the sound of his full name. "Yes."

"You're my page."

"Okay. What do I do?"

"If I fall in battle, you have to see that your mother gets paid."

Will grinned. "Do I forge your signature on a check?"

Austin handed him his wallet.

To Anna's dismay, Will looked inside. His eyes widened and he muttered his usual, "Wow!" Though Anna could be considered wealthy, she'd never flaunted it, and Will received a modest allowance.

"Oh, for heaven's sake," Anna said, simultaneously impatient and excited. "You're supposed to be here to offer a serious opinion on armor for the wedding your fiancée is putting her heart and soul into, and you're playing the Black Knight!"

"Everyone's always telling me I don't play enough," he said, moving toward the middle of the room where Gordon was squaring off. The other two artisans left their work to stand on the sidelines and watch. "And I never buy a product without testing it first."

Anna groaned.

Will patted her back. "He'll be all right, Mom. He used to box in college."

"This isn't boxing," she replied. "This is hitting someone with a heavy ax! Come on. We're not watching!"

"Mo-om!" Will resisted her efforts to draw him away, his eyes riveted on the men beginning to walk around each other, both smiling broadly.

And once Austin started to move, she couldn't take her eyes off him.

The boxing might not have affected his performance with the broadax, which appeared to take two hands to control, but it lent a certain grace and agility to his backward leaps when Hal Gordon attacked.

Anna couldn't help but notice Austin's nicely contoured hips in gray slacks, his muscled thighs when he strained forward to block a blow, his ridged arms when he raised the ax overhead.

Will shouted encouragement when Austin struck a blow that caught Gordon off balance and allowed Austin to move forward. His forward leaps seemed to owe more to some knowledge of fencing rather than boxing, but in a moment Gordon was fighting to avoid being driven farther back.

They held each other to a tight space for several moments, circling, blocking blows, occasionally landing one on a shield. The sound was loud and curiously greeted with laughter by the combatants.

Will laughed, also. Anna decided that amusement under such circumstances had to be a male thing. She waited nervously for someone to lose a limb or be rendered unconscious.

Both men were breathing heavily when they finally decided to call it a draw.

"This thing is warm," Austin said as Hal Gordon separated the breastplate from the backpiece and Will ran up to help hold the armor. "I hate to think how it will feel in August."

Gordon nodded. "True. But in winter it holds the cold, too, so be glad it's not a winter wedding." He asked one of the men on the sidelines to bring Austin a towel. Perspiration ran down both men's faces.

Will and Austin helped Gordon rid himself of the armor while the conversation turned to boxing and the infamous Tyson-Holyfield fight.

Anna put a hand to her eyes. She'd just watched two men fight with medieval weapons in the interest of the Lamont-Cahill wedding. Obviously she'd crossed into an alien reality.

CHAPTER SIX

ANNA LOWERED HER HAND to find Austin watching her, his color high and his eyes bright as he dried his hands. "We're ready to talk business," he said with a grin. "You want to join us?"

"If you're sure *you're* ready," she said sweetly. "I mean, you don't want to joust first, or anything?"

He tossed the towel over the shoulder of his white sweater. "Isn't that what you and I do all the time?"

Danger, Will Robinson! "I'm just trying to plan a wedding," she said.

"So am I," he replied equably. "My bride wants armor, you were fearful of wasting my money, so I made sure the armor was worth the price."

"Are you expecting invaders at your wedding?"

"With Caroline Lamont, who knows what'll happen next. Will?"

Will handed him his wallet. "Here you go, your grace. Or is it your lordship?"

"Not sure." Austin put an arm around Will's shoulders and led him toward Gordon's office. "Meanwhile, you can call me Austin."

"No, I can't," Anna heard Will say, his voice diminishing with distance. "Mom says I have to call you Mr. Cahill."

Austin shook his head. "Then I think I like your grace better."

IT WAS DARK when they left the Gordon Armory with the four suits of armor paid for and scheduled to be delivered to Anna's office the following day.

Will pleaded to ride home with Austin. "Please, Mom!" he begged, hands folded and raised in supplication. "Austin and I...Mr. Cahill and I have lots to talk about."

She glanced at Austin, who nodded. "I'd like his company. You'll be right behind us so you can keep an eye on us."

Austin drove sedately to the outskirts of Austin and she followed, trying to concentrate on the road rather than the pervasive memory of him dancing around the armory floor, flushed and laughing and decidedly sexy.

Then she saw his right turn signal blink.

She sat more attentively and frowned, then groaned as he turned into the parking lot of a fast-food restaurant. She had no choice but to follow and pull in beside him.

Will climbed over the seat and into the back, beckoning her, then patting the front seat to indicate that he'd vacated it so she could join them.

"You didn't tell me you intended to stop," she complained to Austin as she slipped into the passenger seat. She closed the door, enfolding the three of them in an intimate bubble.

"It was a spur-of-the-moment decision," Austin said with no sign of regret. "Will said he was hungry, so we stopped. But we're not going to find you a salad here. Will you settle for something else?''

Will leaned over Austin's seat, his face alive with happiness and excitement. He was a good-natured child with a positive attitude and a cheerful aspect, but she seldom saw him with such boyish delight. She couldn't deflate his joy in the moment.

''Actually,'' she admitted, ''I have a real weakness for their bacon burger with fajita fries. I never indulge it, but I guess I could this once.''

''Can we eat in the car?'' Will asked.

Austin leaned against the door to look at him. ''Won't you be more comfortable inside?''

''And we have to consider the upholstery.'' Anna ran a hand over the rich leather.

''No, we don't,'' Austin corrected. ''It's treated and wipes off.''

''All the other kids,'' Will said eagerly, ''get to go to fast-food places and eat in the car 'cause their baby sister cries or their dog can't go in or something, and I always thought that was so cool—that your family's so big and noisy you have to eat in the car. Usually there's just Mom and me. Or Grandma. Or the whole family goes out, but it's to some fancy place where they serve water and you get a linen napkin to put in your lap.''

Anna saw a touchingly empathetic look cross Austin's face as he reached backward to ruffle Will's hair. The gesture made putty of her backbone.

Then he briskly asked for everyone's order and climbed out to retrieve their requests.

''Hasn't this been the best day!'' Will demanded

of her, leaning over her seat. "First the armor place, then Austin comes to meet us, now we're all going to have dinner—in the *car.*"

She was shaken by the realization that he felt as though he'd missed something—and it wasn't just eating fast food in a car. She'd spent all his life trying to be everything to him, so that he wouldn't notice he had a father who didn't care about him. And it had worked for a while.

But he was getting older, and though his maturity still hadn't caught up with his genius, it was developing to the point where he understood rejection and deprivation.

And she had deprived him of a father.

But she had to do something about this euphoria he experienced in Austin Cahill's company. This was a dangerous affection, and she had to nip it in the bud.

Austin was marrying another woman specifically for the purpose of having a baby! Anna and Will were not part of that package, and she feared her son was beginning to think they might be. Or could be.

She had to make sure he understood. But she couldn't do it now, while he was so thrilled with the moment. She would wait until they were home.

"Let's play that game," Will suggested after Austin returned with the food. He dunked the tip of a French fry in a small paper cup of ketchup. "You know, that one where you start a word with the last letter of the first guy's word?"

Anna nodded. "Austin, you go first."

"Hamburger," he began appropriately.

"Royalty," Anna contributed.

"Oh, sure! Give me a *y*." Will fell back against the seat in pretended dismay. "Um...Yolk!"

"A yoke of oxen or an egg yolk?" Austin asked.

"I don't know." Will grinned at his mother. "Which letter's harder?"

"Probably the K," she replied.

Austin frowned at her. "I'm your client. You're supposed to be on *my* side. Particularly now that I've lived through combat and can pay you. Kettle!"

"Electricity."

"No!" Will groaned. "Another *y*. Ah...the *other* yoke!"

Austin laughed. The game went on until they'd finished their food and Will and Austin were down to sharing the rest of Anna's fries.

"I wish we didn't have to go home," Will said with an extravagant sigh. "This has been a really great day." He leaned over Austin's shoulder to give him the small bag with the last French fry in it.

Anna felt Austin turn in her direction, but she didn't dare look at him. She didn't want him to see even a trace of what she felt—that she wished the day didn't have to end, either.

"Have you thought any more about the puppies?" Will asked.

Austin popped the fry into his mouth then crushed the small bag into the large one that held the rest of their trash. "I did, as a matter of fact," he said.

Will leaned over a little more.

"I looked over their records for the last couple of

years, and the company just needs too much input. It's been failing for too long.''

"But the puppies..."

"Will be fine," Austin insisted. "I'm selling it right away. Whoever buys it will have to be someone really interested in animals because they won't be buying it as part of another company."

"But...you always take good care of everything you buy."

"When it can give me a good return," Austin replied patiently. "Dogdom can't do that."

"But sometimes having a loss is a good thing, isn't it? I mean...it gives you something to deduct."

Austin shook his head. "The loss wouldn't amount to much, Will. Because the company doesn't amount to much. That's why I'm getting rid of it."

Will fell silent while Austin stepped out of the car to throw away the bag of trash.

Anna reached over the seat to touch her son's face. "It's all right, Will. He's probably right about someone buying the company who likes dogs. I'm sure he knows what he's doing—in a business sense, anyway. Do you want to ride home with me?"

Will shook his head. "No. I forgot to ask him about that toy company you and Aunt Beth were interested in investing in."

"Okay." Anna opened her door. "But don't bring up the pet stores anymore, okay? I know you don't agree with what he's doing, but you really don't have the right to question him like that. You're a very smart boy, but he's a respected businessman, and he doesn't have to answer to us. Okay?"

"Okay."

Will climbed into the front seat as Anna got out of the car and locked his door. She pointed through the window to the seat belt, which he obligingly put on.

"Want us to follow you this time," Austin asked over the top of the car, "so we don't make any more unscheduled stops?"

"There's no place else to stop," she said. "We're about five blocks from my home. But you don't know where that is, do you? And you have my son, so you'd better follow me."

"He's mad at me, isn't he?" he asked soberly.

She shook her head. "Just disappointed."

"It's business," he said, then grinned wryly when he apparently remembered the last time he'd used that as an excuse. "God," he muttered teasingly, coming around his car to open her door for her. "I *am* going to hell."

She smiled thinly as she slipped behind the wheel. "Maybe you'll get lucky and Saint Peter will understand the concept. He *was* a fisherman—a man of business."

"That sounds hopeful."

"Unless, of course, he had a dog. Then—"

Austin raised a hand to prevent her from finishing. "I get the picture. You dangle salvation in front of me, then you snatch it away. Not nice, Anna. Not nice at all."

He pushed her door closed and walked around his car.

She found it hard to think of that neat backside going to perdition.

WELL, THERE WAS no denying it, Austin thought. He was in a hell of a fix.

He was developing a thing for Anna Maitland. He didn't want to think it was a problem because he knew himself. It wouldn't come to anything.

It was just a sexual thing.

Sort of.

So far in his life he'd known a lot of beautiful, sexy and frivolous young women. And beautiful, sexy, driven women who had all the appeal of another guy in a dress.

But he'd never met a woman who was caring, intelligent, focused, maternal and still somehow so serene. In the slight tilt of her head, in the delicious roundness of her breasts and hips, in the slender fingers with which she gestured, smoothed Will's hair, tugged at her earring—she was an elemental woman, all grace and confidence and charm.

For one quiet moment as he pulled up behind her at a red light, he wished he'd found her before he'd asked Caroline to have his child. He let himself think about what that might be like—Anna and him, their baby and Will.

Then the light changed and she drove on and he did, too, leaving the thought behind where it belonged—with the red light. He couldn't offer love and he imagined she would never settle for anything less.

Still…it had been nice to think about.

But he had to get his mind off it. He followed the taillights of her car up a side street, then glanced at Will. "You're not talking to me," he observed. "You're mad about the pet stores."

"No," Will said. "Mom told me not to bring it up again. I was just wishing...."

The boy hesitated. He looked troubled.

"Wishing what?" Austin prodded.

Will played with his fingers. "I probably shouldn't say."

"You can say anything to a friend."

"Can you? Even if you're wishing for something that probably isn't...you know...right?"

"Well...wishing for something that isn't right isn't the same as doing it. What are you wishing for?"

"I wish you were marrying my mom," Will said in a quiet voice, "instead of Miss Lamont."

Okay. Well. That destroyed what little reason he'd been able to maintain concerning his own similar thoughts. But he knew it was impossible and he had to make the boy understand that, too.

"Your mother," he said, following her car down a narrow, tree-lined lane into the woods, "needs a man who can give her lots of time and attention and all the wonderful things she deserves to have. I'm...too busy with business."

"She had fun with you today."

"I'm her client. She has to be nice to me."

"No, she doesn't. She told you you were going to hell, remember?"

He laughed at that and felt a little bit of his customary balance restored.

"She did, didn't she?"

"My father wasn't very good to her."

"I've heard that."

"And he doesn't like me."

"She told me he hasn't even taken the trouble to know you. I think that's a big mistake on his part, and I've only known you for a couple of days."

Will smiled at him. "You do?"

Austin found himself wishing for a couple of minutes alone in a locked room with Will's father.

"I do. You know, my father used to drink a lot when I was a little kid. And even though he was around, it was almost as if he wasn't there because he was either drunk or sleeping. I used to think he drank and slept because he was trying to get away from me. Then I figured out as I grew up that it wasn't really me he couldn't deal with. He ran away—in one way or another—from anything that required him to do something hard, or something that he didn't want to do. So if your father can't handle the responsibility of being there for you, it's his fault and not yours. You understand that?"

"I'm trying to," he admitted. "Mom tells me that all the time. Where is your dad?"

"He died when I was eight."

Will patted his arm in a touchingly consoling gesture. "Do you *really* understand it? I mean, about your dad?"

Austin pulled in beside Anna in the back of a sprawling multilevel home lit by floodlights that picked out a broad deck surrounded by decorative shrubbery. He squinted against them, thinking that he hadn't really understood it until this moment. Probably because he wanted so much for Will to understand it.

"Yeah, I think so. It's hard to understand because

it means I was less important to him than the comfort of escaping in alcohol or in sleep. But that's the truth. And the truth is the truth, even when it's ugly.''

Will digested that for a moment, then heaved a deep sigh. "Mom says I should think about all the people who love me instead.''

"She's right," Austin said. "And you can count in one more.''

Will reached over the console to hug him.

Austin felt the crumbling of the long-standing barrier between himself and anyone who tried to get too close.

He hugged Will, keeping a feeling of abject terror to himself.

As Austin and Will emerged from the car, Anna looked warily from one to the other. "Is everything all right?" she asked.

Will nodded. "Everything's fine. Except that the day's over.'' He turned formally to shake Austin's hand. "Thank you for dinner. That was really fun.''

"You're welcome. I had a good time, too.''

"Can I go in while you say good-night?" Will held his hand out to his mother.

She put her keys into it and he hurried to the house, leaving Austin and Anna in a puddle of light surrounded by darkness.

Anna watched Will unlock the door and go inside. "*Is* he all right?" she asked Austin.

If you discount the fact that he wants me for a father, Austin thought, *he's all right.*

He wondered what would happen if he told her

what Will had said, how she would react. Suddenly, that was something he needed desperately to know.

Hands in his pockets, he studied her face, thinking she looked tired. With few reserves left for quick thinking, she'd be inclined to be honest.

"He told me he wishes I was marrying you," he said, "instead of Caroline."

She didn't react at all, and her face told him nothing. "I'm sure you told him that you've made a binding promise," she said quietly, "and that I'm not the kind of woman you're looking for."

Apparently he'd underestimated her reserves of quick thinking. But a sudden tightening of the atmosphere between them and the nature of that last remark made him wonder if that wasn't her way to find out what was on *his* mind.

"You're not?" he asked.

"I'd have to be loved," she said, folding her arms and squaring her shoulders, as though she were taking a stand. "I wasn't the first time. And I'd really like to know what that's like. And I'd want to be loved for me, not just for my ability to reproduce."

Okay. She had him there. She'd have to be loved, and he just wasn't doing that anymore. It was more than a fear of being hurt again, it was a reluctance to be that vulnerable. When he'd loved Lauren, he'd loved so much that it had impaired his judgment. His holdings were now so large and complicated that he had to be in top form just to stay even.

It had come down to a choice for him. Love or business. Wait till Saint Peter heard that one.

He grinned. "Then maybe you'd just let me adopt Will."

Laughter bubbled out of her, then she looked sad—almost as though she regretted his admission that she wasn't the type of woman he was looking for.

"The Fair Trade Commission probably wouldn't allow it," she said. "The two of you could rule the world."

Then without warning—perhaps because she hadn't even known herself that she was going to touch him—she put her hand to the sleeve of his sweater. "Thank you for dinner. Will had such a good time."

A charge went straight to his heart, as though she'd used defibrillation paddles on him.

He saw her eyes widen and guessed that the charge had kicked back.

She dropped her hand instantly, looked first disoriented and then angry, then turned to go.

He caught her hand, the charge ricocheting inside his body. He didn't understand it but couldn't ignore it. He pulled her toward him.

The anger was gone from her eyes, and she looked sad. "Austin, don't even think about it!" she whispered.

"I'm not thinking," he said, still pulling, "I'm just doing."

The night was cool, the air redolent of pine and the promise of spring. The wind sighed and the leaves whispered, and something shouted inside him. *Don't let her go!*

She let him draw her into his arms until they were

body to body and he could see himself reflected in her eyes. Her upturned face was pale and perfectly sculpted, and her bottom lip gave one betraying quiver.

Then she firmed it and wedged a space between them with her hands against his chest.

"You're engaged," she reminded him quietly.

At the moment, he wondered what colossal stupidity had led him to do such a thing. "You know the circumstances."

"I do," she agreed, still pushing. "But my son doesn't, and he's probably watching from his bedroom window."

It took every particle of self-control he possessed to drop his arms. All he wanted out of life at that moment was to pull her closer and taste her lips.

But her son, who thought Austin was the savior of the world, or at least of a passel of puppies, was watching.

"Can you admit to me," he asked, "that there's something here?"

Her eyes met his honestly, filled with whatever that something was. It couldn't be love, could it, if he wasn't able to give it and she wouldn't let him even if he could?

"It would be foolish to deny it," she said finally. "But that doesn't mean anything."

It shouldn't, but it did. "I can't explain it," he said, "but though it doesn't alter the situation, it means everything to *me*."

She drew a ragged little sigh. "I have to go."

He needed so much to touch her again, but he didn't. "Good night," he said.

She gave him a brief parting glance filled with confusion and condemnation and turned toward the house.

Austin glanced to the second level and saw that she'd been right. Will waved to him from the middle window.

He waved back, then got into his car, feeling for the first time in his adult life that he'd lost his direction.

"HE LIKES YOU." Will wrapped his arms around Anna's neck as she leaned down to kiss him goodnight half an hour later. Unlike the rooms of most boys his age, his was not papered with posters of sports heroes, but with photos of businessmen he admired and sports cars he intended to buy one day when he was successful. Anna now recognized one very handsome face right over his dresser as Austin Cahill.

"He'd better," she replied, avoiding his eyes as she pulled up his blankets. "He's my client. And we have a lot of work to do together."

"I don't mean like a client." Will seemed determined to make his point. "I mean like…a girlfriend. A woman friend. What do you call it when people who are older love each other?"

"If one of them is engaged to someone else," she said briskly, folding the top of the sheet over his blankets, "it's called cheating. And we don't allow that in this family."

"But it isn't smart to marry somebody if you like somebody else better, is it?"

It seemed clear he wasn't going to drop the subject without an explanation. She sat on the edge of his bed. "Sometimes people get married for other reasons—things they think they need more than love—and it works out just fine."

He raised both eyebrows. "What could you need more than love?"

"I'm not sure, but his life is all about business rather than family, so he must need something else." She wasn't about to try to explain Austin's desire for a baby.

Will folded his hands behind his head. "He said that *you* needed someone who could give you lots of time and attention and all the good things you deserve."

She shook her head as she realized what had probably prompted that reply. "He told me what you said about wishing he was marrying me."

Will propped himself up on his elbows. "He asked me what I was thinking about and I told him I probably shouldn't say 'cause it might not be right, but he said thinking about something that was wrong was different from doing something wrong, and that friends could tell each other anything!" He said all that without taking a breath, the last few words coming out strangled.

"Okay," she said calmly, pushing him gently back to his pillows. "I didn't mean to sound critical, but that embarrasses me, Will. You have to understand that he's going to marry Miss Lamont, and that he and I are just two people who are trying to plan a wedding together while she's gone. Nothing romantic is going to come of this. I know that disappoints you, but you're not getting a father out of this, okay?''

Will folded his arms belligerently. "He said he loved me."

"He did?"

"We were talking about my dad and... Did you know that his dad drank too much when Austin was little and that it felt just like he'd left?''

She remembered Austin had told her that and began to understand how her son and his idol had become so close so quickly.

"Yes, he did mention that.''

"Well, I told him that you said I shouldn't think about Dad not liking me, that I should concentrate instead on all the people who do love me.''

"That's right.''

"He said that I could count one more.''

Anna caught his hand and squeezed. "Of course he loves you. Everyone loves you. You're a wonderful person. But he's going to marry Miss Lamont and they're going to have their own family.''

He shook his head. "No, they're not. They're just going to have a baby, then she's going to go away.'' When Anna reacted with surprise that he knew those details, he added, "Whitney told me after I went back to the day care. Her mother is friends with Miss Lamont and thinks that isn't a good thing to do.''

"Maybe it isn't," Anna said, "but Austin and Miss Lamont get to do whatever they want with their lives as long as they don't hurt anybody else. And their lives are none of our business, except for the wedding I'm helping them plan.''

He stared moodily at the ceiling, then he sighed and seemed to relax. "Okay," he said finally.

She was suspicious of his sudden capitulation.

"That means you're just humoring me, doesn't it?" she asked with a smile, tucking him in as though he were two. "And you're going to believe what you want to believe."

"I know more about him than you do."

"Well, I know more about why people get married than you do."

"But he always gets what he wants. Every company he's gone after now belongs to the Cahill Corporation."

Anna leaned over him, a hand on either side of him, and said gently but emphatically, "He's marrying Caroline Lamont, so that must be what he wants."

Will met her eyes. "It was—until he met you."

"If you say that one more time," she threatened, "I'm selling you to the Gypsies."

"Then who would handle your investments?"

"I'll do it myself."

"Maybe I can find someone else to live with when you lose everything."

"Or I might sell you to recoup my losses." She kissed him and turned off his light. "Good night, Will."

"'Night, Mom."

"Love you."

"Me, too."

She stopped at the door, feeling she had to give it one more try.

"It's wonderful to dream," she said, "but pinning your hopes on things that just can't happen wastes a lot of energy."

She hoped for agreement, but expected argument. Instead, she got evasion.

"Good night," he said.

She smiled to herself as she pulled his door half closed. She shouldn't be surprised that he was stubborn. He was a Maitland, after all.

CHAPTER SEVEN

ANNA HURRIED into Oh, Baby! the following Monday, determined to put all thoughts of Austin Cahill and her son's adoration of him out of her mind. It was cowardly, she knew, but she had no idea what to do about her son or her client. And she had a million other details to take care of that she could handle with some confidence, so it seemed only reasonable to tackle them first.

At the top of her list was shopping for a shower gift for Connor and Janelle's baby. Her mother had seen that little Chase lacked nothing since she'd found him on the hospital's doorstep, but Anna was determined to locate just the right gift. Then she had to be at her office in time for the delivery of Caroline's armor in the afternoon.

She took a circuitous route through the shelves of stuffed animals and headed for the counter to ask Lana Lord, the owner and her good friend, for help. Perusing the colorful plush toys was for her own enjoyment; the baby already had a stuffed zoo.

Noticing that Lana was busy with a customer, Anna stopped for a second look at a particularly engaging gorilla the size of a large toddler. He held a stuffed kitten in his arms as though it were a baby.

"A wonderful maternity hospital," Lana was saying. "It has a sterling reputation and I can honestly say, since I know ninety percent of the staff and administration, that it's deserved. I'm sure your daughter would be well-treated there."

"Wasn't there something of a scandal several months back," a strong male voice asked, "about the paternity of a baby found on the hospital steps? Didn't it belong to one of the clinic's staff?"

"No," Lana replied. "That was simple speculation that proved false."

"Then who were the baby's parents?"

"There is a couple who've claimed him, but Megan Maitland still has guardianship of the baby until the records of the birth arrive."

"Mmm. Megan Maitland. The clinic's CEO. What do you think of her?"

Anna was becoming annoyed. The man certainly was nosy for the father of a prospective patient. She could understand his wanting reassurance about the hospital's performance, but the family questions were going a little too far.

Lana, a great fan of the Maitland family and practically a member herself, seemed happy to sing Megan's praises.

As she did so, Anna peered around a giant plush elephant to identify the customer. She got a view of him in profile as he wrote a check at the counter.

He wore elegant, casual clothes, probably a cashmere sweater and boots that had the distinctive mark of a custom creation. Tall and slender, he was nicely bulky in the shoulders and moved with a style that suggested either breeding or a firm conviction of his self-worth.

Anna admired his confidence and was annoyed by it at the same time because he reminded her of Austin.

Lana was placing a fuzzy honey-colored bear in a box filled with tissue. Strains of "The Teddybears' Picnic" drifted through the store.

"Megan bought this same bear for that baby," Lana said as she placed the lid on the box. Then she moved down the counter to the roll of gift wrap affixed there. She pulled out a foot of colored paper and tore it perfectly with the cutter edge. "She took that little fellow in like he was her own. She did the same for my sister and my brothers and me, you know. We were foundlings, too."

"Really," the man said. His check written, he leaned an elbow on the counter and watched her work.

She proceeded to tell him the whole story of how Megan, with a large brood of her own, found a home for the abandoned foursome.

"She cares about everybody."

"Ah," he said. "A socialite out to save the world?"

That did it. Anna stormed to the counter, ignoring Lana's look of wide-eyed surprise.

"Who are you?" she demanded of the man, who straightened as she approached. "And what right do you have to interrogate Lana about the Maitlands, and then express insulting opinions about my mother that clearly prove you haven't listened to anything Lana's told you?"

His lips twitched, and she thought he might smile. He should consider himself lucky he didn't.

"I'm Harrison Smith," he said, extending a hand toward her. "Which Maitland are you?"

Lana began to speak, presumably to make introductions, but Anna silenced her with a glance.

"You didn't answer all my questions," she said to Harrison Smith. "You've told me your name, but not who you think you are that you can *investigate* my mother and the rest of my family—"

"Whoa!" He held up the hand he'd offered. "I *was* asking questions about the hospital, but my daughter's going to be a patient there, and naturally I was interested in the family because the hospital is mostly run by Maitlands, isn't it?"

"Yes, it is, and very well," she replied, lowering her voice a fraction. "And since there are a lot of us, I'd be careful what I said for fear of being overheard. My brothers are pretty big."

He did smile then. "And some of you are pretty scary without being big. Are you Abby, the ob-gyn my friend recommended to me for my daughter?"

She shook her head. "That's my sister. I'm Anna."

He looked her over in a way that was not at all sexual, but simply assessing.

"Anna's a wedding planner," Lana said brightly, obviously hoping to lighten the atmosphere. "Are you married, Mr. Smith?"

"Not anymore," he replied. "I don't think I'll be needing Anna's services anytime soon."

"Me, either," Lana said. The box wrapped, she turned it right side up, peeled the back off a bright yellow bow and affixed it to the top. "Though I'd like to very much." She sighed philosophically and handed the box to Smith. "But the world's full of people you can't trust, people who can stomp all over your dreams and keep going like nothing ever happened. You have to be careful."

"Amen," Smith said feelingly. "Beautiful package. Thank you very much."

"You're welcome, Mr. Smith. Now, come on." She gestured Anna closer. "Let's start over. I know you two would like each other if you'd met under different circumstances. Anna Maitland, this is Harrison Smith, from…"

"Montana," he said, and offered his hand again.

Anna took it.

"Harrison Smith," Lana went on, "Anna Maitland."

"And do you have children of your own?" he asked as they shook hands.

"One son," she replied.

Smith pointed. "That isn't him, is it?"

Startled, Anna realized she still held a very large stuffed gorilla in her left arm.

"I'm just asking," he went on innocently, "because I thought I detected a certain likeness in the frown."

For a moment Anna couldn't decide whether to laugh or bristle with indignation. She chose to laugh.

Actually, she didn't choose. The laughter just bubbled out of her as she remembered the half smile on his face when she'd approached. She'd presumed it was condescending amusement, but considering she'd been cuddling a stuffed gorilla in her arms, he'd had a very good reason to smile.

"Actually, I'm here to buy a gift for the baby that you were asking Lana about," she finally replied. "And when I saw that Lana was busy with you, I decided to check this guy out a little closer. I didn't realize I was still carrying him."

"You make a great picture, Anna," he said, a curiously nostalgic softness in his dark eyes. Then he picked up his package and smiled at Lana. "Thank you again." He turned to Anna. "And you, too, for having a forgiving nature and a sense of humor."

She sighed and shifted the gorilla in her arms. "Just be careful what you say about my family from now on, or Kong and I are coming after you."

He smiled. "I'll be careful. Ladies." He inclined his head and walked out of the store.

"Whew." Lana took the gorilla. "Please. No violence while you're carrying my stock. He certainly is gorgeous, though, isn't he?"

"Yes," Anna had to admit. "But he's a Nosey Parker."

"I think he was just concerned for his daughter," Lana decided. "He didn't mean any harm."

"He called Mom a socialite."

"She is a socialite."

"I don't think he meant it in a good way."

"Oh." Lana put the gorilla on a corner of the counter and took a picture frame from behind her. "He was just curious, that's all. Had he been asking about someone else's family, you wouldn't even have noticed. How about this for the baby." She held up the frame and fiddled with something on the back. Anna stared at it in surprise as the image changed from kittens in a basket to puppies in a flower bed. "It's the newest thing, called a Spaceframe." She held up what looked like a little wedge of plastic. "This is a chip that contains twelve different images that'll change every thirty, sixty or ninety seconds, or every couple of hours, depending on how you set it. Or you can take photos of the family with a special camera, take the film to a photo lab, and instead of getting prints, you get one of these little wedges with your photos on it. Isn't that cool?"

"I like it," Anna said. "But I'd prefer something a little...cuddlier."

"The gorilla?"

"I don't know. Help me look until you get another customer."

Lana came around the corner to join her, a smile on her lips. "You promise not to attack the next one?"

AUSTIN WALKED from his hotel toward town with no particular destination in mind. He'd received a call from Caroline this morning telling him that the fashion show had gone well, but that her sister, Camille, was still under the weather and she wanted to stay with her for a few days to try to help her recovery along.

"Of course," he'd said, "but Anna has a few questions for you about the menu and the music for the reception."

"I trust you to make those decisions," she told him, then when he fell silent, shocked that she was willing to leave those details to him, she added, "or you can give her this number, if you'd rather I talked to her."

"Are you all right?" he asked. She sounded a little frail.

"I'm fine," she replied. "I may have a touch of what Camille has."

"Well, take care of yourself," he said.

"I'll be fine. Did you find armor?"

"We did. And we're going to use my horses."

"Oh," she said, as though such a practical solution had never occurred to her. "I never thought of that."

"That's why we have a wedding planner."

"Right. I'll call you tomorrow and let you know how it's going."

"All right. Take care."

"Yes." She sighed. "You, too."

There was a small hesitation—a little hole in their conversation that another couple might have filled with, "I love you."

But Caroline simply said, "Bye, Austin."

He answered, "Bye, Caroline."

He prowled along Mayfair Avenue, feeling as though that hole in the conversation represented a giant hole in his life. And for the first time since he'd approached Caroline a month ago about getting married, he wondered if a baby would fill that void.

Then he reminded himself that that wasn't why he wanted a baby. It wasn't intended to fill his needs. He was the one who would share the fruits of his success with another human being. This baby was about giving, not getting.

He had to admit that he was vain enough to like the notion of a boy who looked like him, thought like him. Or of a little girl with his eyes and his business savvy.

He liked the notion of a child like Will Maitland.

But his baby's mother would be Caroline Lamont and not Anna Maitland, so there really was no possibility of his offspring having that touchingly sweet personality Will had.

Jamming his hands in his pockets, he kept walking, overcome by a mood weirdly composed of sadness and an anger he couldn't justify or define. Maybe a coffee at the diner just ahead would help him shake the feeling.

Completely lost in the complexity of his emotions, he collided suddenly with something large and wooden, and saw stars.

Flinging his arms out, he tried to regain his balance and stop the world from spinning.

He heard a high gasp, a strangled cry, a deep-throated, pithy oath, then a familiar female voice exclaim in dismay, "Oh, my God! Ellie, what did you *do?*"

While he fought to clear his head, arms wrapped around him and pulled him off to one side. There were more than two arms. It felt as if there were two on each of his, and a hand was touching his face, exploring the place on his forehead where he'd been struck.

Either he was surrounded by women, he thought a

little wildly, or one very fragrant and chagrined wind-mill.

Then a firm pair of hands—male hands—pushed him onto a bench and someone sat beside him.

"I didn't do it," a woman's voice replied. "Beth did it."

"Only because Mitchell pushed me out the door!"

"He was nowhere near you!"

"Somebody shoved the door open for me!"

"Will you stop fighting?" That was Anna's voice, Austin was sure of it. Where the hell was he? "We've practically knocked one of my clients unconscious! Mitch, is he okay? Does he have a concussion?"

"Cahill?" he heard a male voice say. "What's he doing here?" Fingers pried Austin's eyes open. "Can you hear me? What's your name?"

"I can't believe this. Austin? Can you hear me? How many fingers do you see?"

Two slender fingers, nails glossed with a clear pol-ish, appeared in front of his eyes. Behind them he had a fuzzy picture of Anna's face as she bent toward him. She was flanked on either side by a pair of female faces that looked remarkably like hers.

"Hey," the man beside him said to her. "Which one of us is the doctor?"

"Well, *do* something!" Anna demanded. "His forehead's bleeding!"

"Sis, it's just a scratch. Cahill? Can you hear me?"

Austin drew a breath and felt the world settle into order. He saw Anna more clearly and identified the worried, anxious look on her face. That pleased him inordinately.

"Yeah," he replied, putting a hand to his forehead. "And I saw two fingers. I was just...walking. Thinking. I saw...a familiar neighborhood and...what happened?"

Anna's hands settled on his in his lap, and she squatted in front of him, looking into his face with great concern. "We were celebrating the fact that we all had a free hour at the same time, then we realized Ellie was late getting back to work, so we hurried out and I...*I* pushed the door too hard and hit you in the face. I'm so sorry. Are you all right?"

"Yeah." For a moment he couldn't tear his eyes from the anxiety in hers. Then, to convince her that he was fine, he looked around, saw beautiful female twins, probably in their mid-twenties, and a man with strong features seated beside him.

The man smiled and offered his hand. "Mitchell Maitland," he said. "Let's take you to the hospital and have a closer look at you."

Austin shook his hand, then stood to prove that he could. "Thanks, but I'm okay. There's no need to—"

"Nonsense." Anna stood also and took his arm. "We're taking you to the hospital and that's final. Mitch, will you help me? Austin, Mitch is my brother. Do you remember him from the day of the hostage situation at the day care? And the two warring princesses are my sisters, Beth and Ellie. You met Beth that day, too."

With both of Anna's arms wrapped around his, Austin didn't have the heart—or the desire—to protest any further. He became part of a small parade that marched up the street to the maternity hospital's emergency room.

"You're right—I think he's fine." Abby, another attractive Maitland and an ob-gyn, nodded at Mitch, who had called her in to have a look at Austin. "I'll bet your friends and family tease you about your hard head," she joked with Austin. "Now you can tell them it's come in handy."

"You're sure he's okay?" R. J. Maitland had heard the commotion when they arrived and followed them into the examining room to see what was going on. "If word got out that *we* injured Austin Cahill…"

Anna rolled her eyes. "R.J., *we* did not injure him—I did. I don't intend to tell anyone. And I don't think Austin intends to sue." She focused on him with sudden gravity. "You don't, do you?"

"Of course not."

"Good!" she said triumphantly. "See, R.J.? No liability to the hospital, so you can relax." Then she looked startled and glanced at her watch. "Oh, my God! My armor! It's due any minute!"

Her siblings looked at one another as she gathered her purse and suit jacket, left on a chair.

"Your armor," R.J. repeated.

Abby reached out to put a hand to her sister's head.

Anna gave R.J. a look and swatted Abby's hand away. "It's a long story. Austin, do you feel well enough to come with me and make sure it's all arrived safely?"

He'd been hoping for such an opportunity.

"I do." He leaped off the examining table, thanked

Mitchell and Abby, then glanced over the assembled group. "Is this all of you?"

R.J. shook his head. "We have another brother, Jake. He's…somewhere. We never know from day to day. He's a free spirit."

"Seven. Quite a family."

R.J. smirked. "You don't know the half of it."

Anna held on to Austin's arm as they left the hospital and walked up the street to her office. He slowed his step sufficiently to convince her that he needed her support.

"I'll make you a cup of coffee as soon as we get upstairs," she promised. "Did I mention how sorry I am?"

"Eleven times," he replied with a smile he hoped looked wan. "I counted."

"I have a chaise you can rest on until you have to pick up Caroline. Or would you like me to do that for you? Her flight comes in at—"

"No flight," he said as they waited for the elevator. "Her sister's still feeling punk, so she's staying an extra couple of days."

"Did you ask her about—"

He cut her off as the elevator doors parted on an empty car and they got on. "She gave me a sort of groom's power of attorney to make decisions."

Anna looked as stunned as he had felt at the time. "She did?"

"Or I can give you her sister's number and you can call her there."

"Well…it's your wedding, too," she said warily. "But she's been so specific about what she wants.

I'm afraid if she gets back and doesn't approve, it'll be too late to fix it.''

He nodded. "I'll give you the number.''

WHEN AUSTIN REFUSED to recline on the fainting couch, Anna sat him in her desk chair and talked nonstop, telling him about the caterer she'd found who could do a medieval feast, the seamstress who called to say the costumes were progressing fabulously and Anna would have them in a couple of weeks, and the florist who promised lilies and roses to decorate the hall and wildflowers for the attendants and for Caroline's coronet.

She knew Austin saw through her chatter to the nervousness underneath. What he didn't know was that his presence had such a power to undermine her control that when she'd opened the door on her way out of Austin Eats, she'd caught sight of Austin through the small, square window in the upper half, and an involuntary jerk of her arm and a slight loss of balance pushed the door right into his face.

She didn't understand what was wrong with her. She'd been unaffected by men for the past ten years, and the last thing she wanted right now was to find herself attracted to one. Particularly this one, who was engaged to someone else—*and* a client!

Well, maybe she had a glimpse of understanding into why she had this reaction to him.

She wanted to be held.

She wanted to be touched.

She wanted a man to look deeply into her eyes and

tell her that he loved her and she would never be lonely again.

Turning her back to Austin, she went to the window as that realization created a sinking feeling inside her.

This couldn't be menopause already, could it? Impossible. She'd been taking hormone replacement therapy for three years. This wasn't the result of estrogen imbalance or mood swings.

Mercy. This was serious interest. Sexual interest. Worse than that, it was sexual interest sparked by a fascination with all aspects of the man. It felt like the first bud of…love.

Love.

Great. She'd chased it as a young woman, misidentified it in John, decided to live without it for ten years and finally discovered it in someone she couldn't have.

Wasn't life amusing?

A hand on her arm brought her out of her thoughts with a jolt, and she spun around to give Austin a sharp push backward. She regretted it instantly, remembering that she'd only recently given him a blow to the head. She was relieved to note that he held his ground with relative ease.

His blue eyes looked surprised for a moment, then he seemed to relax, as though understanding what had prompted her action.

He pointed beyond her to the delivery van on the street below. "I was just going to tell you that the truck's here."

"I'm sorry," she said, squaring her shoulders and tugging down the jacket of her suit. "I...I—"

He cut her off with a shake of his head. "No need to apologize. I understand."

She folded her arms, trying to create a distance between them with an imperious attitude. "Do you?" she asked coolly.

He smiled, but thinly. "I do," he insisted. "I'm always aware of you, too."

She was caught off guard by that simple admission and dropped her arms.

"Excuse me," he said. "I'll see if I can lend them a hand."

An hour later the office of Wonderful Weddings looked like Agincourt before the battle. The four suits of armor, lined up two on either side of a decorative escritoire, had been highly polished and delivered in perfect condition.

Anna lifted the protective visor on the more decorative of the suits and peered inside. It smelled of iron and polish.

"I wonder what it was like in there," she said, "with arrows flying and other people falling around you."

"Frightening, I'm sure," he replied. "I think I'd prefer to be more vulnerable to injury if it meant I'd have more freedom of movement."

"Unless you had a family waiting at home, needing you to return safe and sound." She closed the visor and stepped back to look at the suit. "Then I suppose you'd protect yourself as much as possible to make sure you got home."

"I suppose you would," he agreed, standing right beside her. Then he asked mildly, "How long are we going to talk about empty suits of armor instead of us?"

She sent him a warning glance. "'Us,'" she reminded him, "is you and Caroline."

"No," he corrected. "Caroline and I have always been she and I, never *us*. And...I'm not so sure anymore that that's a good idea."

In an odd and purely selfish way, she was happy that knowing her had made the legendary Austin Cahill rethink his decision to marry a woman with whom he'd bargained for an heir. But it was one thing to entertain a selfish thought and quite another to behave in a selfish way.

It was time to put a stop to this.

She turned to him, her arms folded and her jaw firm. "Look, Austin. By your own admission, you can't love anyone. And I've already been married to a man who didn't love me and I hated it. So your great wealth does not have sufficient appeal to me to make me consider getting mixed up with you. I'm a wealthy woman in my own right. I don't have a fraction of your wealth, but I have enough for Will and me to be very comfortable and for Will to go to an Ivy League college and set himself up in any business he chooses. And besides, Caroline is my *client*. I would never deceive anyone in that way even if I *didn't* know them."

He listened to her little speech with a calm expression, then said, "I'm not talking about deception. I'm talking about admitting right out loud that from the moment we met, there was something between us that's grown considerably over the last week and refuses to submit to my plan to marry Caroline and your duty to us as our wedding planner. It wants acknowledgment. It demands honesty."

"All right," she admitted boldly. "I acknowledge that I find you attractive. I did that the other night."

"It's more than attraction," he said quietly. "It's already past that for both of us."

She pursed her lips in what she hoped was a show of determination. "Whatever it is," she replied stiffly, "I'm having nothing to do with it, and you're marrying Caroline Lamont."

He studied her closely, looking, she was sure, for the feelings she was battling. She turned away. "I think you'd better go."

He turned her toward him, holding her still with the slightest pressure on her arms. He dipped his head to look into her eyes. "And I think you'd better face the truth here, Anna."

Before looking at him, she made her expression a careful blank. "You're engaged to Caroline, that's the truth. Will takes all my time and attention. That's another truth."

He looked at the ceiling impatiently, then at her again. "How long have you been doing this?"

"What?"

"Deluding yourself into thinking that all you are is working woman and mother. Did you let your ex-husband do that to you?"

She raised her arms to break his hold. "No one *did*

it to me. It's who I am. I've been a wife and a lover and I didn't like it."

Her action didn't work. He firmed his grip on her. "But he didn't love you."

"You wouldn't love me. You said so yourself!"

"No," he corrected patiently, "I said I hadn't been able to love anyone since Lauren." He shrugged and smiled suddenly, as though what he was thinking surprised even him. "But...I don't seem to feel that way anymore."

The words gave her both a shock and considerable pleasure, then she remembered the reality of her position.

"Maybe," she said feebly, "you've fallen in love with Caroline, and you're just confused because I'm here, and she...isn't."

He gave her a small shake. "Anna! Who would ever confuse the two of you?" His voice was half annoyed, half amused. "You're warm and solid and a wonderful mother. Caroline's a great person, a good friend, but—" he lowered his voice as though the feeling was too strong for sound "—she's not what a man dreams of in a woman."

She fought the temptation to slip right into his arms. He didn't know everything. Probably couldn't imagine...

"Mom!" Will burst through the door, schoolbooks in one arm and waving a note in the other hand. He stopped short at the sight of Austin with his hands on her, his expression first hopeful, then, when he noticed her grim expression, concerned. "What happened?" he asked.

I have to put this wonderful man out of my life, she replied silently, *and I hate it.*

Aloud, she said, "I was just...feeling a little faint. Austin was here looking at the armor—" she indicated the lineup of suits "—and was just about to lead me to a chair."

Okay. The story was thin, but on the spur of the moment and in her rattled state of mind, it was the best she could do.

Austin, for his part, walked her to the desk chair and helped her into it. But she saw Will and Austin exchange a look over her head—man language, she guessed, for "We'll talk later."

Will disappeared into the back room and returned in a moment with a bottle of water.

The thoughtful gesture restored Anna's control. "Thanks, Will. I'll be fine. What do *you* think of the armor?"

He went to inspect it more closely. "I think it's weird for a wedding," he answered, "but they're really cool. I bet they were heavy to wear."

"I think so," Austin agreed conversationally. "And the weapons were so heavy you'd have to be pumping iron all the time to have the muscle to fight."

Will knocked lightly on the arm of the closest suit and at the resultant clang turned to smile at Austin. "I guess when you wore one of these, raising your arm would be considered pumping iron."

Austin laughed. "You got that right."

"Will you come to Fathers and Careers Day with me?" Will blurted. He folded and unfolded his arms, a bright blush rising from his shirt collar. The request had clearly been hard for him to make. "Those of us who don't have dads," he explained, his voice a little raspy, "can bring an uncle or a friend."

"Sure," Austin replied without hesitation, an answer that both delighted and alarmed Anna.

She was pleased that Austin had agreed for Will's sake. She knew how much her son idolized him, and how important he would feel in front of his classmates because he'd brought such a well-known businessman to the event.

But from her perspective, she'd been just about to tell Austin that she didn't want to see him until the day of the wedding, that she'd run all her questions by Caroline, and he could just stay out of her way.

"What about Mothers and Careers Day?" Anna teased.

"That's next month," Will said.

"When is the fathers thing?" Austin asked.

Will came toward him, staring in disbelief. "On Friday. You'll really come?"

"Yes," Austin replied. "I'd like to."

"You have time?"

"Sure."

"'Cause Mom said when you first came that you were really busy planning the wedding, and you had to work from here and there wasn't even time to meet me. But then we had that thing at the day care and we sort of met anyway, but I didn't think you'd ever be able to..." Will realized suddenly that he was chattering and put both hands over his mouth to stop the flow of words.

Austin patted Will's shoulder. "Yeah, well, a lot's changed since then."

Will dropped his hands and followed Austin to the door. "Did anybody buy Dogdom yet?"

"Will," Anna warned.

"I was just asking," Will said defensively.

"Not yet," Austin replied. "So, you'll call me the night before the careers thing and tell me where I'm supposed to go?"

"We'll pick you up!" Will volunteered excitedly. "Mom always takes me to school. We'll come and get you. Right, Mom?"

Anna forced a smile. "Sure."

"Great! Mom, I'm gonna walk Austin down to his car, okay?"

"Fine. But come right back."

Austin hesitated at the door only an instant, letting Will precede him into the hallway, but it was long enough to give Anna a look that told her their argument wasn't over.

When the door closed behind them, she muttered a profanity she wouldn't have said in front of her son, and opened her appointment book to check tomorrow's schedule.

CHAPTER EIGHT

"I THINK we should wait by the door!" Petey whispered harshly, pushing up the band of the black woolen watch cap that kept slipping into his eyes.

Janelle, crouched behind him and also wearing black, rolled her eyes. "Petey, use your head! There's a floodlight on top of the restaurant door. You make a move there and everybody going by will be on top of us."

He pointed his knife to the empty street. "What people going by? It's ten o'clock at night. This part of town is buttoned up tight."

Janelle jerked the knife back. "No, it's not! And will you keep that out of sight! The clinic is right up the street. People are coming and going all the time."

Petey huffed impatiently. "Well, how long are we supposed to wait in a Dumpster? This isn't what I had in mind, you know, when you promised me a rich family, big bucks and a future of leisure."

"Petey, you are such a wuss," Janelle grumbled. God. The man was a marathoner in bed, but give him a little discomfort, and he whined like a two-year-old. "You're not *in* a Dumpster, you're behind one. And I know it doesn't smell great, and I know you'd rather be watching the big-screen TV in Megan's family room, but in order to have the rich family, the big bucks *and* the future of leisure, we have to get rid of Lacy."

"Well, where the hell is she?"

She opened her mouth to tell him where she wished *he* was, then decided that she had to try another tack. If they were going to get rid of this obstacle in their path, she had to get him to stop moping and concentrate.

They were crouched together behind the Dumpster, and she rubbed his knee. "I told you, Petey, you just have to be patient."

He groaned. "I'm not a patient man, Janelle. You know that. How long have we been at this now?"

"It's only been half an hour."

"No, I mean this scheme! It's been months! I'm getting antsy. Why don't we just steal Megan's money and get the hell out of here?"

"Because if we're patient," she explained, "we'll get Megan's money, and everything else that's coming to that little brat."

"Yeah," he muttered dryly. "And we'll have to take the kid, too."

She shook her head. "He's our ticket to ride, baby. Now come on. Pay atten— Listen! Here she comes!"

Janelle's heart began beating with a frenzy as she heard footsteps walking out of the restaurant, the firm closing of the door, the rattling of the knob to make sure it was locked.

Beside her, Petey firmed his grip on the knife and squatted tensely, waiting for Lacy Clark to walk past.

Janelle counted Lacy's steps as the gravel crunched beneath her feet. Six, seven, eight.

Her heart pounded. Petey turned to look at her, his eyes menacing in the darkness. She felt the energy in him, the grimly eager anticipation.

Nine. Ten. Eleven.

She was getting closer. Another step and she'd be there beside them—the perfect target.

Twel—

"Sara! Sara, it's Anna!" a female voice shouted across the dark lot, filling Janelle with rage as she yanked Petey down.

He'd leaped up, planning to attack anyway, and though Anna wouldn't have seen them from where she sat in her car at the curb, it still would have been disastrous. If she'd seen Sara clearly enough to shout at her, then she could see her disappear.

Petey tried to fight her, but she held on for dear life, trying to still her heartbeat enough to hear the conversation.

"Anna!" she heard Lacy cry. "What are you doing here?"

There was the sound of a car door closing, and Anna's voice, loud and clear.

"Will and I made an ice-cream run. You just leaving?"

"Yes. There was a little extra cleanup tonight. Our busser was sick."

"Well, let me take you home."

"I can walk—or catch the bus."

"Come on. It's on our way."

"Thank you, Anna." Lacy's voice grew quieter as her footsteps crunched toward the car.

"After we do Lacy," Petey said with dark determination, "Anna's next."

"You shouldn't be walking home at this hour of the night." Anna found Sara's face in her rearview mirror and frowned. "It isn't safe."

Sara shrugged. "Until I can buy a car," she said, "I have little choice."

"Maybe you could carpool with someone at the hospital," Anna suggested. "The swing shift leaves about the same time you do."

"I'd hate to impose on a stranger. Everyone I know has been so kind to me already. And it's really not such a long walk."

"Why don't we just lend her money for a car?" Will asked.

Sara gasped, then laughed nervously. "Absolutely not!"

Anna glanced at her son with a smile as she pulled up at a Stop sign. "What a brilliant idea, Will."

"No!" Sara insisted. "It would take me an eternity to pay you back. My future is uncertain, I have no idea if I already have any bills or debts or—"

"We'll write easy terms." Anna interrupted her. "Like, you can pay me back when you can."

Will grinned over his shoulder at their passenger. "Or you could pay us back in chicken and dumplings!"

The argument continued until Anna pulled to a stop in front of Mrs. Parker's Inn, the boardinghouse where Sara lived. "I had a client who owns an auto agency," Anna said. "I'll set up an appointment for you. You don't have a license, do you?"

"Mom." Will met Anna's eyes, humor shining in his. "If she had a license, she'd know what her name is."

Anna accepted that proof of her faulty reasoning skills with equanimity. She was getting used to her child being smarter than she was.

"True," she said. "Okay. We'll have to take you for your test, then find you insurance."

"Anna..."

"I'll let you know about the appointment when I come to the restaurant for lunch tomorrow."

"Anna..."

Will climbed out of the car and opened the back door for Sara. Anna complimented herself on her son's good manners. They were either attributable to her example or to the fact that he'd been smitten with Sara since the first time he saw her at Austin Eats.

Sara tried to argue further, but Anna shooed her toward her building. "Good night. We'll sit here until you're inside."

With a shake of her head, Sara ran gracefully to the double glass doors and let herself in.

Will grinned broadly as Anna pulled away from the curb and headed for home. "I think she'll be happy," he said, "when she stops being surprised."

"I think so, too."

"Good surprises are great. Like Austin being able to come to Fathers and Careers Day."

"Right." For all the personal distress he caused

her, she considered it a nice surprise that a man she could have loved existed—even if he was about to marry someone else.

ANNA DISCOVERED the following morning, however, that he was less convinced of that than she was. He was leaning against her office door when she arrived.

She stopped halfway down the hallway at the sight of him, her pulse picking up at the lazy, graceful way he straightened and turned toward her. He looked wonderful in jeans and a dark blue sweater over a chambray shirt.

"Good morning," she said, continuing toward him, trying to steady her voice and her hands and appear in control. She had keys in one hand, a cup of coffee in the other and her purse tucked under her arm. "You're not conducting business today?"

"Actually, I'm here on business," he said, taking her coffee from her while she unlocked the door.

She turned the knob but paused to look at him worriedly before pushing the door open. "Don't tell me Caroline's changed her mind about the medieval theme now that we have four suits of armor?" Finding a use for garden umbrellas was one thing. Full suits of armor were something else.

"No." He pushed the door open for her. "I am picking her up at the airport today, though, so who knows what could happen when she gets here. But I'm on personal business."

"Austin, don't start," she pleaded, walking into the room and trying to leave him as far behind as possible.

He seemed to be cooperating, stopping just inside the door after closing it behind him. But he had her coffee. For a moment, she couldn't decide which she needed more—the caffeine or the relative peace a little distance from him afforded her.

"Too late," he said. "And don't blame me. You're the one who started it."

She bristled. "I did not."

He was unimpressed. "Maybe not deliberately. The point is, I'm falling in love with you, and it changes everything."

"No, it doesn't."

"And you're falling in love with me."

"I'm not!"

"Liar," he said quietly, and came toward her.

"I'm not!" she insisted again. "And I'm...I'm making a bundle on this wedding, so don't mess it up for me." She took a step around her desk, and he got closer. She pointed to her desk blotter. "Put the coffee down."

He considered the cup of coffee in his hand, apparently realizing for the first time that it was a bargaining chip.

"If you want this," he said, a dangerous note in his voice, "you're going to have to tell me the truth."

"I just did."

"No. That was the truth you'd like to believe. But that's not the truth that is."

"We make our own truths, Austin," she said, grasping desperately for control of the situation. And if he didn't put the coffee down this instant, she could not be held responsible for what became of his brilliant life.

"That's what I'm about to do," he said. "I'm going to tell Caroline I'm canceling the wedding. Then you and I are getting married."

"Austin, you're crazy!"

"Yeah. You coming for this coffee?"

"Put it down."

"Sorry."

"Look." She closed her eyes and struggled for a logical argument. "Even if yours wasn't a love match, Caroline's bound to be disappointed, to feel rejected. You can't just write her off."

"I'm not writing her off." He held the cup up invitingly. "She loves my house in Kauai. I'll give it to her."

"And what are you going to do with four suits of armor, a medieval feast and yards of ivy?"

He smiled. "You can talk your next clients into a medieval wedding and tell them it's already paid for."

"But it isn't."

"It will be." He waggled the cup in his fingers, taunting her with it. "Coffee's getting cold."

She put the words together as convincingly as she could. "I am *not* marrying you, Austin Cahill. You think you're falling in love, but you're just infatuated with something you can't have. Isn't that a typical rich man's reaction to the unattainable? Change a life plan and move heaven and earth to get it? Well, you're not the answer to my prayers, buddy, so get the—"

She stretched an arm out to point to the door as she started to demand that he leave, but he caught her wrist and used it to pull her to him. Once she was trapped in his arms, he put the coffee down.

"Austin..." She pushed against him, guessing what he intended. Wanting it and not wanting it at the same time.

He caught a fistful of her hair in one hand and held just tightly enough to prevent her from moving. "Save your breath," he said, his eyes roving her features with a flattering hunger that quickened her heartbeat. "You just tell one fib after another."

His head was bending closer to hers, and she tried to ward him off with sarcasm. "You can't believe that a woman doesn't want you?"

It didn't work. His lips were a centimeter from hers. "I don't believe that *you* don't want me. But let's see if you can prove it to me."

She was certain it would be easy. After the first two weeks of her marriage to John, she'd felt nothing when he took her in his arms, nothing when he kissed her, less than nothing when he made love to her.

She knew she would feel something when Austin kissed her. She was attracted to him and, despite all her denials, a little bit in love with him. But she wasn't about to let him change his life and hers for something that simply couldn't happen. And that was far more important than whatever reaction her libido had to...

Austin's lips met hers, and her libido made short shrift of her easy dismissal of it. Desire burst out of the heart of her, hot, eager, pulsing.

His other hand moved to the center of her back and held her tightly to him as the kiss went on and on.

She felt as though champagne sparkled in her veins, filling every corner of her with a tingling sensation.

Never before had she been kissed like this. Though she tried to resist him, Austin seemed far more determined to give her something than to take something from her.

She stood still in his arms as he feathered kisses along the line of her throat, across her ears and over her face. There was a tender reverence in the action, a kind of homage that humbled her yet seemed to lend her power.

When he moved to her lips again, she wrapped her arms around his neck and gave it all back to him—the eagerness, the discovery and the passionate tenderness at the heart of it all.

A tiny part of her not completely lost in the kiss understood that she'd just denied feeling any of this and was making a dangerous admission here. But most of her knew only that this kind of connection—soul to soul, spirit to spirit—was everything she'd imagined in her girlish dreams, everything she'd hoped to find in her marriage. Everything that had been denied her—until now.

She realized suddenly that she stood alone except for one steadying hand on her arm. She opened her eyes and saw that Austin looked disgustingly pleased with her response to him.

"You don't love me," he said with a grin as he

handed her the coffee. "Yeah. Right. I'm off to the airport. See you later."

Anna held the cup in shaky hands and took a needy sip. It was still hot.

Geez. And so was she.

AUSTIN SPOTTED CAROLINE instantly in the stream of passengers arriving from Galveston. She stood out like a sunbeam in the rain in a yellow trench coat, her hair curled in a style very different from her usual sleek do.

She spotted him and waved, beaming a wide smile as she fought her way through the crowd to him. Then she threw herself at him and held on, a reaction that both stunned and alarmed him.

No. What was she doing?

She leaned back to look at him, her arms still looped around his neck from the hug. Her gray eyes were bright with something he couldn't define but knew he'd never seen there before. Her cheeks were pink, and she seemed to be lit from inside.

Oh, no. Could it be possible that absence had made the heart grow fonder, like the old adage promised? Because she looked as though...

"I've missed you!" she said feelingly, and gave him a noisy kiss on the cheek. "Can we have a cup of coffee before we go back?"

"Sure. Rough flight?"

She tucked her arm in his and leaned companionably against him as they left the commuter terminal and headed for the escalators that would take them to the shops and restaurants.

"No. I'm just tired. I've hardly slept in days."

"Was Camille that ill?"

"No. There was just a lot to catch up on." She glanced at him with a smile. "Anna left me a message with the details of the medieval feast."

"Did she?" He hadn't known that. Anna's way, probably, of determining that the wedding must go on.

But it couldn't. He knew that with absolute certainty. But Caroline in an affectionate mood was making it extremely difficult for him to broach the subject. He hoped this stop for coffee would give him an opportunity.

But when he sat across from her at a small round table in a crowded little shop, she glowed like a high-wattage bulb, and the words caught in his throat.

She reached across the table to catch his hands in hers and squeezed. "I don't know what I'd have done without you these past couple of years, Austin," she said, her expression sobering. "You're the best friend I've ever had. And now..."

The waitress came.

Austin would have leaned back, but Caroline had a death grip on his hands.

"Raspberry mocha, please," Caroline ordered. "And do you have a croissant?"

"Plain or cream cheese filled?"

"Ooh. Cream cheese."

"Coffee," Austin said. "Black."

The waitress left.

Caroline stared at their joined hands, and he noticed with real worry that her bottom lip trembled.

He couldn't marry her, but she'd been a good friend to him, too, and the last thing in the world he wanted was to see her hurt.

"What is it?" he asked gently.

A tear slid down her cheek, and her nails dug into his knuckles. "We have a major problem," she said finally with a despairing shake of her head.

"Okay," he said in a comforting tone. "I'm sure it's nothing we can't fix."

She looked into his eyes, hers clearly challenging that statement.

"I've, um…" She tilted her head and ran her thumb over his fingernails. "I've…fallen in love."

God help him. Telling her he'd changed his mind would have been hard enough when they'd been merely friends, but if she'd missed him during her trip and decided she was in love with him, then that made it—

His thoughts came to an abrupt halt at the sight of the turquoise ring on the third finger of her left hand. He'd never seen it in all the time they'd spent together.

Suddenly, he realized he might be wrong about the source of her problem.

"You're in love with…?"

"Bobby Blackford," she said, a guilty look in her eyes, but a wistful smile on her lips. She leaned toward him anxiously. "I don't know how it happened. I mean, we were in the French Club in high school, but I thought he was a dork and he thought I was a snot, but he took his mom and his sister to the fashion show for his sister's birthday and he came back to see me when it was over and…I don't know… We just…" She spread her arms helplessly.

Half an anvil lifted off his shoulders. Thanks to the object of *his* affections, the other half remained.

"That's wonderful," he said, lifting her hands to his lips. "I'm happy for you. I really am."

She looked at him, her tear-filled eyes wide with astonishment. "You are?"

"I am. Honestly." He smiled teasingly. "So much for all your claims that you've never known love and don't trust it."

"I know!" she agreed with ingenuous sincerity. "But it was almost like I had nothing to do with it. By the time I noticed, it had already happened and there was no way to stop it. I kept thinking of my promise to you and… Oh, Austin. Can you find someone else to give you that baby? I feel so badly…."

He shook his head. "No need. I was going to tell you that I'd changed my mind and couldn't go through with it."

"You're kidding! Why?"

It was a curiously hard thing to say, he realized, when its outcome was uncertain. "Because I've fallen in love," he said.

Her smile widened slowly. "So much for *your* claim of an unwillingness to love."

He nodded wryly. "Yeah. Aren't we a pair?"

She looked at him closely, a new depth in her gaze he'd never seen before. "Anna?" she asked.

Now he was astonished. Did being in love give you some kind of radar that spotted others in the same state?

"Yes," he replied. "But she says she's not in love with me."

The waitress brought their drinks, and Caroline winked at him. "Poor Anna. Does she know how you react to a challenge?"

He drew his coffee toward him. "She's about to find out."

CHAPTER NINE

ANNA NIBBLED on the small bag of potato chips she'd brought to the office after lunch at Austin Eats. It wasn't like her to eat chips, but she was in a self-destructive mood.

"So, what can you do for me?" she asked the line of hollow knights on either side of her escritoire as she paced back and forth, munching. "Here you are, all prepared for battle, and you're just standing there. I could use a few champions, you know. I'm trying to do the right thing, but all I really *want* to do is throw my arms around Austin Cahill and hang the consequences." She idly lifted a face guard and peered inside. "Well, maybe it's best that you're all as hollow as my ex-husband. If you were to go to battle for right and honor, you'd have to *prevent* me from having what I want."

A swift rap on the office door put an end to Anna's one-sided conversation.

Chelsea Markum, the notorious reporter for Tattle Today TV, was in the hallway when Anna opened the door. A cameraman stood behind her, portable camera on his shoulder.

Anna hated bad manners but was tempted to resort to rudeness. Chelsea had made a spectacle of Chase's arrival on Maitland Maternity's doorstep, and her overly enthusiastic investigation had cast suspicion on Anna's brothers and annoyed and embarrassed everyone.

"Yes?" Anna asked stiffly.

Chelsea smiled. She was tall and leggy with perfect curves and disgustingly gorgeous auburn hair in a chic, short cut. She was also indomitable, and on some level Anna couldn't help responding to that.

"Caroline Lamont called me several days ago and asked me to come and see you for the details of her wedding." She pointed beyond Anna to the office. "May I come in? I promise not to keep you too long."

"Aren't weddings a little off your beat of gossip and scandal?" Anna asked the rude question in a polite tone.

Chelsea didn't seem to notice. "Any other wedding would be, but this one's a little different. Austin Cahill, the legendary bachelor, marrying Caroline Lamont, the perennial princess. I'll bet the prenup alone is newsworthy."

Anna forced herself to think of this from Caroline's perspective rather than her own. Chelsea was good at distributing the news, and Caroline did seem to think her alliance with Austin would have national interest. Fortunately, Anna knew nothing about their financial agreements, so she couldn't even be coerced into speculating.

Heading into her office, she pointed to the suits of armor.

The photographer wandered the room, camera

whirring, while Chelsea took notes on Anna's descriptions of the wedding party's medieval attire, the ivy bower, the flowers, the food. Anna told her about their arrival at the church on horses.

Chelsea blinked. "Horses."

"Horses."

"Sounds like quite a spectacle."

Anna smiled sweetly. "And one you can report on without having to make anything up."

Chelsea fended off her riposte with a smile. "Sticks and stones, Ms. Maitland. Didn't I see you and your son in the company of Austin Cahill at his hotel?"

Except for the second's pause before she responded, Anna did not react guiltily to the question. She felt guilty, though. She was sure her eyes screamed, *I love Austin Cahill!*

"Yes, you did. In the restaurant."

"Miss Lamont was...unavailable?"

"Yes," she replied evenly. "She was in Galveston replacing her sister in a fashion show. You know Camille Lamont?"

Chelsea nodded. "I do. Quite a woman."

"Yes. Well, she's been quite an *ill* woman for a couple of days. Caroline took her place in the show, then stayed with her for several days to help her recover."

"Hmm. Even with all the details of her own wedding to be settled."

"Mr. Cahill took care of them in her absence."

Chelsea Markum looked suspicious. "I can't imagine her leaving those kinds of details to anyone else— even her intended."

Before Anna had to assure her that was indeed the case, the door burst open and Caroline hurried into the room looking vibrant and renewed. She flew at Anna and wrapped her in an enthusiastic hug.

"Anna!" she exclaimed. "How are you? I've missed our little get-togethers. Chelsea! You came!"

She stopped abruptly when she saw the cameraman.

Chelsea asked him to wait for her in the truck.

Relaxing, Caroline wrapped Chelsea in a warm embrace. Anna watched her with fascination and just a little sadness. Her client was in love; her face practically radiated her joy. So. In her absence from Austin, she'd realized that she loved him.

Anna drew a deep breath and swallowed, telling herself this was best for everyone. Caroline's sparkle was bound to convince Austin that he was doing the right thing, after all.

And that would help Anna put him out of her mind.

Caroline and Chelsea had moved to the suits of armor, and Caroline exclaimed over them as she admired the chased details.

"And who's going to be wearing the suits?" Chelsea asked, turning her recorder on and holding it up. "Neither Austin nor you has brothers, am I right?"

Caroline ran a hand over a breastplate. "No one's going to wear them," she said.

"Ah. They're going to be propped up in front of the church so that it looks like someone's in them?"

"No." Caroline smiled apologetically at Anna, then at Chelsea. "There's not going to be a wedding."

Chelsea stared at her.

"What!" Anna demanded.

Caroline came over to Anna's desk, dropped her purse on it and fell into the client's chair. "No wedding," she repeated. "Austin and I talked this morning at the airport, and it's over."

"No!" Anna shouted, feeling as though the world was tumbling off its axis.

"Anna..." Caroline began calmly.

"No!" Anna insisted. "You can't do that, Caroline! Don't listen to him!"

"Listen to—" Caroline frowned in perplexity, but Anna didn't notice. She was intent on singlehandedly righting the world.

"You listen to *me!*" she said firmly, shaking her finger at the stunned woman in the chair, unmindful of the reporter wandering closer, the tape in her recorder still turning. "Austin's wrong about this! The kiss didn't mean anything! It was just that he was confused, I think, and I...I don't know what happened! I think I've just wanted the right man all my life, but he was never there, and I spend all my time making everybody else's alliance come together in just the..."

She chattered on, trying to explain the unexplainable, then realized that Caroline stared at her in smiling surprise and Chelsea in greedy delight.

She stared back, finally understanding that Caroline hadn't known about the kiss, probably had no idea what she was talking about, and that Chelsea was thrilled with this latest tidbit of gossip.

Anna closed her eyes and prayed for beam-up or divine lightning—she'd have been grateful for either.

But the moment stretched on, and she continued to stand there embarrassed and horrified.

To her complete shock, Caroline rose out of her chair and wrapped her arms around her again, laughing. Then she held her at arm's length.

"I was going to say that I ran into an old boyfriend in Galveston and that we fell in love. I broke off the wedding, Austin didn't. In fact, he was going to come with me to tell you, but he got a call on his cell phone. Some kind of emergency in his L.A. office." She smiled slyly. "He told me he was in love. So, what's been going on while the cat was away?"

For someone who was chattering like a maniac a moment ago, Anna couldn't think of a thing to say in response to Caroline's announcement.

Caroline was in love with someone else?

"Anna," Caroline said gently, "I've never known Austin to act on emotion. If he kissed you in a way that makes you look like..." She turned to Chelsea. "How would you describe that?"

Chelsea grinned. "I don't know. Paradoxical, I guess. She looks radiant, and she looks terrified."

Caroline seemed to concur. "I'd say he really cares for you," she said. "And stop denying that it meant anything to you. You look like a halogen light."

At Anna's stupefaction, Caroline hugged her and laughed once more, then pointed toward the suits of armor. "Do you think you can help me transport all this to Las Vegas?"

"HI, *DARLING*. I have to fly to L.A. this afternoon, but I'll call you from there tonight. I wanted to come with Caroline to explain what happened, but the problem in L.A. is urgent and I'm taking my jet right out. I won't be more than a day, though. Love you. Hi, Will! We have a lot to talk about."

Anna stopped in the middle of the living room, a stack of mail in her hands, paralyzed by the endearment spoken by Austin on her answering machine.

Will came out of the kitchen, a half-eaten banana in his hands, his eyes the size of headlights. He swallowed an apparently large bite of banana. "What did he say?" he gasped.

She ignored the little glow Austin's words gave her and continued to look through the mail. "He went to L.A.," she said matter-of-factly. "You're going to spoil your dinner, Will."

"No, what did he say before he said he was going to L.A.?"

"I didn't notice."

"He called you *darling*." He gave the word a dramatic emphasis.

"I didn't notice."

"What about Miss Lamont?"

Anna sat on the sofa because the state of her knees required it, then sorted the mail into three piles. "She fell in love with someone else while she was in Galveston."

He came to sit beside her. "In four days?"

"It was someone she knew before." She handed Will an advertisement for a financial magazine.

"So now you can have him?" he asked frankly. "I

mean, now it's not cheating because he doesn't belong to anybody else.''

She put the mail down and leaned against the back of the sofa, the beginning of a headache throbbing between her eyes. "No, I can't, Will. Because he just wants to marry me because he wants to have a baby.''

He turned to face her as he chewed and swallowed another bite of banana. "But that's not bad, is it? The guys say, you know, sex is pretty neat.''

She turned to him, a new worry getting in line with all the others. "And what do they know about it? Please tell me no one in your class has firsthand experience.''

He tossed his banana peel on her carved bench cum coffee table. "Chip Dumas tried to tell us he did,'' he said, clearly doubtful, "and that he did it with a condom. But he can't even get them open to make water balloons, and none of the girls like him 'cause he burps and stuff. So I don't think it's true.''

"And what about the rest of you?''

"Books and movies, mostly,'' he said. "And some stories from Ricky Gerber's older brother. He says it makes you feel great.''

Anna tried to turn her mind from the thought that ten-year-olds were discussing sex and to remember that she had to make a point here.

"If you have it with someone you love,'' she said, giving him her full attention, "it can be pretty wonderful. But if you fool around with it when you're too young or just eager to experiment, it can have major consequences.''

"Right," he said knowledgeably. "Babies. So, you've never had it be really great, I guess."

"What?"

"Sex."

How did conversations with Will always become unmanageable? she wondered. Then she saw the genuine concern in his eyes and realized that it was unmanageable only for her. And it didn't have to be.

"No, I haven't," she replied frankly. "I had high hopes for it, and at first, when I loved your father and I thought he was in love with me, it was...nice. Not really great because he was sort of..." She struggled for words that would put John's selfishness delicately.

"He probably didn't make sure that you had a good time, too, did he?" Will asked candidly, shocking her. "Ricky's brother says it's better all around if you make sure the lady's happy, too."

She could only hope Ricky's brother hadn't gone into extensive detail on how he accomplished that.

"That was pretty much it," she admitted. "I felt as though he liked sex just because. Not because he was having it with me."

"I'll bet Austin wouldn't be like that."

"He wants sex just to have a baby," she reminded him. "You want cocoa?"

"Depends."

She stood and headed for the kitchen. "On what?" she asked as he followed her.

"On if you're making it just so I'll stop asking questions." He smiled when he spoke, his eyes teasing.

Catching his neck in the crook of her arm, she applied a noogie to the crown of his head. "I can't believe," she said, freeing him as they reached the kitchen, "that a kid who knows so much still has so many questions."

He sat on the counter beside her as she brought down cups, a teabag for her and an instant cocoa packet for him.

"I just really like him, Mom." His teasing smile grew wider. "Come on. I try not to ask you for anything. Can't I have just this one thing? A dad for me would be good for you, too. Sometimes he could drive me to stuff and you could relax. And maybe he cooks! Did you ever think of that? And I bet he knows how to fix stuff so we don't always have to call Uncle R.J. or Uncle Mitch."

She filled the kettle under the tap, then put it on a rear burner and turned it on.

"He's so busy with his company that even if he did know how to do that stuff, he wouldn't have time." She kissed his cheek and tweaked his nose. "You're not getting Austin Cahill for a father, Will, and that's final."

"To you, maybe," he said with a sigh. "But that message sounded like it's not final to him."

Austin called as promised after Will had gone to bed, but Anna let the answering machine take the call. At least, that had been her intention. But Will picked up the phone.

Feeling a little guilty, she listened in on the living room extension.

"Hey, Will," Austin said cheerfully. "How'd your day go?"

"Not bad," Will replied, his voice exuding excitement and affection. "How was yours?"

"Half good, half bad. I wanted to have dinner with you and your mom tonight, but one of my vice presidents, a good friend of mine, had a heart attack and I had to come out and make sure he's being taken care of."

"How's he doing?"

"Very well. It wasn't as bad as they thought at first, and he's in good health otherwise, so I think he'll be okay."

"So that was the half bad stuff."

"Right."

"Was the good stuff that Miss Lamont decided to marry someone else so you can have Mom now?"

Anna forgot she was eavesdropping. "William Maitland," she began in a warning tone.

"I guess I have to say good-night," Will said to Austin. "Are you coming home tomorrow?"

"First thing," Austin replied with a laugh. "Hi, Anna. Bye, Will."

"Bye, Austin. Good night, Mom."

"Good night, Will. Austin. I'm sorry he—"

"What? Spoke the truth? Nothing to hold back anymore, my love. No one to deceive or upset. You can be honest about what you feel."

"I have been, Austin." She sounded cool, convincing. "You and I are not going to happen, even if Caroline is marrying someone else. Surely you have another friend who'll provide you with a baby."

"I don't want a friend. I want you."

"Well, you can't have me."

"Why? That kiss was proof that you care."

"Yeah, well, I've been married and you haven't. Caring's a pretty small word when it comes to forever after."

"You're afraid I'll turn out to be like your ex?"

She wasn't. She couldn't lie, but she had to be more creative in her denial. "No, you're not at all like John. But we don't want the same things out of life, Austin."

"I want you and you want me, even though you insist you don't. What else is there?"

"For one thing," she said, "we aren't in this alone. I have a son who adores you, but as busy as you are, not only would I never see you, but he wouldn't, either."

"I can make some changes there."

"And they'd only last until the next crisis when the only one who could solve it is you."

"You're borrowing trouble, Anna."

"Austin, listen to me!" She sounded more forceful than she'd intended, then put a hand over her eyes and sighed.

"Okay," he said patiently. "I'm listening."

"I don't want more children," she said before she could find a more delicate way to put it. The words hung there on their cross-country connection, silence at both ends of the line.

AUSTIN HEARD the words in complete surprise and wasn't sure what to make of them. They'd been clear, emphatic, precise. He wasn't sure why he didn't believe them.

Maybe because he was a little obsessed about the idea of a baby. But she already had Will. She'd been through the agonies of sleepless nights, complete loss of privacy, a schedule altered to fit that of the baby. And she had an active business that required her time and energy. Of course she wouldn't willingly forfeit that to fulfill his dreams.

"Even with help?" he asked. "A nanny?"

"No."

She said that emphatically, but he'd come to detect every subtle nuance in her voice over the last week and he heard something there that didn't match the meaning of the word.

He could challenge her on it, but she was strong and determined; he knew where that would get him.

Difficult as biding his time was for a man accustomed to taking action, he decided that was the only way he was going to win this one.

"Okay," he said finally. "I've got a deal going in Austin, and Will's thing at school. I'll be back to the hotel in the morning, so I'll be around for another week, anyway. Call me when you decide you want to tell me the truth about this. I'm still ready to listen. Good night, Anna."

He hung up on the startled sound of her gasp.

WILL WAS very quiet over breakfast. Anna felt reasonably sure he'd eavesdropped on her conversation with Austin and was not happy with her end of it. She would have tried to explain it to him, but she hadn't slept all night and felt less than fresh. And, after she dropped off Will at school, she was supposed to pick up her mother, Janelle and the baby to register Janelle and Connor for wedding gifts.

Rojalia, her rotund and warmhearted housekeeper, could usually be counted on to leave Anna in peace over her second cup of coffee while Will ran upstairs to get his things for school.

But this morning she hurried into the dining room excitedly, tugging on Anna and pointing to the kitchen.

"Meeses Anna, the television!" she said in heavily accented English. *"Rápido!"*

Anna let herself be pulled into the kitchen, expecting to find a blank screen or static snow. But the problem was much worse. And the television, unfortunately, was working just fine.

Chelsea Markum had a small segment on Tattle Today TV morning news magazine show as well as her own program. And there she was in flattering blue, talking about someone's glamorous fiancée being out of town.

"She say Matrimonios Maravillosos!" Rojalia exclaimed excitedly "You, *señora!* Wonderful Weddeengs!"

"So I ask you, viewers," Chelsea said with a wicked look at the camera, "which cool king of the conglomerates was charming Austin's foremost creator of Wonderful Weddings, hmm, with lunch at his hotel and a mysterious trip to a remote spot in Elgin? Lucky break, of course, that his fiancée returned home from her own glamour trip, only to break off her wedding to said cool king, leaving the court free for..." She smiled coyly. "What do you suppose? A wedding or a merger? Don't worry. I'm keeping an eye on it for you.''

Anna closed her eyes and would have given anything for the option of going back to bed. But she had to take Will to school. And she had to meet her mother.

Just wait until Chelsea Markum came to her for wedding planning. She would bring back the old tradition of having the wedding couple leap over a broom—and it would not be for tradition's sake, but because Anna was chasing her with it.

Rojalia looked puzzled at Anna's distress.

"Free...*cómo se dice?* Advertising!" When Anna continued to look grim, she asked doubtfully, "No?"

"No," Anna confirmed, knowing Rojalia hadn't understood the entire context of the "free advertising."

Will arrived, backpack in place, and snagged his lunch off the counter. "I'm ready," he declared.

So am I, Anna thought. *For several months in Borneo.* Headhunters were less of a menace than Chelsea Markum.

"WHAT WERE YOU *thinking?*" Megan demanded twenty minutes later. Anna had left Will at school and stopped to pick up her mother. They stood with the baby in the rose garden, waiting for Janelle to join them. "You were fooling around with a *client?* And Austin Cahill, at that? While his fiancée was off working for charity? Anna..."

"Mother," Anna said firmly, fighting her despondency so she could defend herself. "First of all, the trip to Elgin was to buy armor for the wedding, and he met me there *because* Caroline was out of town and couldn't come herself. Her sister was sick, she stayed a few extra days to help her, so Austin was the only one I could ask to make decisions about the wedding.''

"And lunch at his hotel?''

Anna rolled her eyes. "For heaven's sake, Mom. We were talking about the food for the reception. And Will was with us. Who could possibly think of that as clandestine?''

Megan continued to look suspicious. "Chelsea Markum is ruthless with her gossip, but more often than not there's a grain of truth that triggers it.''

"So, you'd rather believe her than me?'' Anna plucked the baby from Megan's arms and nuzzled him as he laughed. "Here, boo boo. Let me get you away from your dotty grandmother.''

Chase took her chin in his hand and tried to remove it.

"I believe you,'' Megan said after a moment, her eyes scanning Anna's face with maternal radar. "But there's been something different about you the last few days. I've noticed it. R.J.'s remarked on it. Even Ellie mentioned it to me.''

"Having a crazy family,'' she said, making faces at the baby, "usually shows on a person.''

"Something about a tall, handsome man whom you knocked unconscious with the front door of Austin Eats?''

"I slipped. He happened to be in the way.''

"Mitch said he saw you jolt at the sight of him and

fall into the door. He said you were very solicitous of this gentleman. A certain Austin Cahill?''

"Of course I was solicitous. I didn't want him to croak before he'd paid me.''

Megan shook her head at Anna. "You were always such a self-protective little fibber. What happens now that Caroline Lamont is marrying someone else?''

"Nothing,'' she replied without meeting her mother's eyes.

"Why not? And don't lie to your mother.''

"Because he was marrying Caroline just to beget an heir. How selfish is that? I've already had one selfish husband.''

"That's true,'' Megan said. "But it wouldn't have anything to do with—''

"No.'' Anna knew where she was going with the question and cut her off. "Nothing.''

"Here I am!'' Janelle exclaimed, running out of the house and down the path in a short, snug red wool suit. "Hi, Anna! Come to Mama, Chase baby.''

Janelle took the baby, ignoring his cries of protest, and headed for Anna's car. "I'm so excited about getting to pick out things,'' she said. "My mama never had anything new, you know. All hand-me-downs and secondhand things. I'm going to love getting presents!''

Anna wasn't sure if she was just in a bad mood from finding herself in the news that morning, or if Janelle was beginning to wear on her a little. Something about the entire situation was making her feel edgy and out of sorts. And it was strange that after all this time with the baby, there seemed to be no bonding taking place. Chase still didn't like Janelle.

"I forgot about the car seat," Anna said as she opened the door for Janelle.

Janelle dismissed the problem and climbed in. "Oh, I'll just hold him on my lap."

"It's against the law," Megan said. "We'd better get the—"

"Oh, honestly!" Janelle settled comfortably into the front passenger seat. "It's just half a mile to the mall."

"But if something happened…"

"What could happen?" Janelle asked. Then with the smallest note of acid in her still playful voice, she added, "Anna's driving. Nothing bad ever happens when Anna's in charge."

Anna caught her mother's eye and saw the same curious confusion there that she felt.

"You're right about that," Anna said lightly. "That's why we're taking Mom's car, after all. It'll be easier than moving the car seat." Anna held her hand out to her mother for her keys. "I'll drive, though."

"I can drive," Megan said even as she handed over her keys.

"I know." Anna beeped open the doors and left Janelle to follow as she helped her mother into the front seat. "But I've never gotten a ticket for doing eighty in a residential area."

"I explained that. I was late for bridge."

Janelle climbed into the back with Chase, placing him in the car seat. "My goodness," she said. "Such a fuss for a short little ride. Does somebody have PMS today or something?''

As Anna drove, she congratulated herself on having restored her good humor. If she hadn't, she'd have turned around and punched Janelle in the nose.

CHAPTER TEN

JANELLE HAD the Mayfair department store in an uproar. Shoppers and staff alike were crowded around her to admire the baby, and though Chase didn't seem wild about his mother, he did respond to the attention from everyone else with coos and giggles and flailing arms.

"You can't really fault Austin for wanting a baby," Megan said as she and Anna studied stemware a small distance from the crowd. "When you and R.J. came to us, he was already hell on wheels, but you were the sweetest, dearest thing. I never tired of watching both of you learn and develop.

"But you grew so fast, I wanted to have another baby, then another and another." She smiled—a little wistfully, Anna thought. "And now you all make my old age a delight." Megan grinned. "A little tumultuous, but delightful. And what a wonderful surprise to find Connor again."

The concerns Anna felt about her long-lost cousin sprang to mind, but she didn't want to spoil her mother's nostalgic mood.

Chelsea Markum had appeared, sans cameraman, presumably on a shopping expedition. But Janelle made the most of the moment and beckoned Megan to her, as though to point out their family togetherness.

Anna longed for an antacid.

While Janelle, Megan and the clerk discussed the merits of stoneware for everyday dishes, Chelsea slipped away.

Anna pretended interest in a crystal pitcher, hoping to avoid the woman who'd made her part of the morning news.

"Good morning, Anna," Chelsea said cheerfully. "You're looking well."

"Thank you," Anna replied, smiling blandly. "Since I unexpectedly found myself on breakfast television, I thought I'd better be prepared for the resultant attention."

Chelsea came to stand beside her, studying a set of tumblers with exotic threads of color blown into the glass. "I think you and Austin would make just the baby he wants. Caroline's beautiful and fun in her way, but you have substance as well as beauty."

"Forgive me, Chelsea," she said with strained patience, "but how can you justify broadcasting someone's personal and private need to procreate as a juicy tidbit for your viewers to digest with bacon and eggs?"

Apparently accustomed to the criticism, Chelsea nodded. "Caroline made no secret of why he was marrying her. It's news. And my morning spot didn't mention that I considered you a better mother candidate than Caroline, only that I thought you were now in the running."

"Well, I'm not."

"Well, I think you should reconsider. He's really quite a guy. He does things for charity no one knows about. He's helped all kinds of people in all kinds of ways and kept it out of the press. He's a very decent human being. I've covered many events he's attended, and I've never seen him look at another woman the way he looks at you."

Flustered, Anna moved to put the pitcher back but missed the glass shelf.

Chelsea acted quickly and caught it at waist level. While Anna put a hand to her thudding heart, Chelsea replaced the pitcher.

"Thank you," Anna said grudgingly.

Nodding, Chelsea hooked an arm in hers and led her toward the linens. "Can we talk for a minute?" she asked.

"Depends," Anna said. "Is it going to make tomorrow's spot?"

Chelsea ignored the remark. "Are you convinced that Connor and Janelle are genuine?"

The desperate need to share that concern with someone outweighed her annoyance with her companion. "No, I'm not." She sighed. "But I think my mother's had them investigated."

Chelsea looked at Megan, Janelle and the baby. They were standing around a display of flatware with the salesclerk pointing out various items.

"Something about them makes me uneasy," Chelsea said.

Anna nodded. "Me, too. But I can't prove anything."

"So, you don't have a problem with my looking into their backgrounds?"

"No. But I just told you I think it's already been done."

Chelsea smiled. "Not by me. I'll let you know what I find out."

"On the morning news?"

Chelsea accepted that gibe with good humor. "I guess I owe you that one. I'll be in touch."

Anna finally returned the car keys to her mother and took a cab to her office in time for a lunch date with a client who didn't show up.

And that was why she lay stretched out on the fainting couch, a box of candy open at her side, when Austin arrived. She was tired of everyone and everything and feeling generally quarrelsome.

He rapped lightly once and walked in, smiling indulgently when he found her. She'd kicked off her shoes, and her stockinged legs were crossed at the ankles. She tugged a little self-consciously at the skirt of her black wool dress.

"No appointments today?" he asked, coming to sit on the edge of the couch near her feet.

"One—" she tucked her feet up, out of his way "—but they didn't show."

He caught her ankles and pulled them in place. "Changed their minds about getting married?" he asked.

She wanted to answer, but her mind was filled with the sensation of his warm, strong hand wrapped around both her ankles. She felt the heat all the way to her heart.

"Um...no." She considered the chocolates so she wouldn't have to look at him and possibly reveal in her eyes what she felt. "They're...in their eighties. They occasionally forget things."

Mercifully, he moved his hand but placed it on the couch on the other side of her legs so that she was trapped. "What if they forget the wedding?"

"The bride's daughter's coming to help." She selected a truffle and bit into it greedily, hoping for a sugar rush. Now that Austin was here, she was not only depressed, but frustrated, as well.

"What's the chocolate for?" He unbuttoned his jacket and leaned lightly against her legs.

She pretended not to notice. "It's for me," she replied.

He laughed softly. "I see that, but *what* is it for? Having a bad day?"

"I spent the morning with my mother and my cousin's bride, registering Janelle for wedding gifts."

"I thought you liked your mother."

"I do. But I'm starting to have trouble with Janelle."

"What do you mean?"

She popped the second half of the truffle into her mouth and shrugged as she chewed and swallowed. Then she shared the fears she had about Janelle and Connor.

"Her own baby doesn't like her," she said, then could have kicked herself for having mentioned the word. She waited for him to use it as a springboard for an argument about their relationship, but he didn't.

"That happens sometimes, doesn't it?" he asked

conversationally. "Mothers and babies take a while to bond?"

"In this case a very long time, I guess. I just have this...feeling."

"Mmm. Well. I've always been of the opinion that you should trust those feelings. Why don't we check them out?"

"Actually..." She glanced at him guiltily and picked out a nut cluster. "Chelsea Markum is going to do that."

"I see." His hand moved to gently caress her calf. It was the most erotic sensation she'd ever felt. "I understand you've made us a news item while I was out of town."

She dropped the chocolate into the box and drew her legs out of his reach. She put the box on the floor and swung her legs over the side of the couch until she was sitting up.

"It was an accident," she explained with a sigh. "Chelsea was here wanting details about the wedding plans when Caroline walked in and told me the wedding wasn't going to happen. I thought you'd told her you thought you were in love with *me* because of that kiss, so I told her the kiss didn't mean anything." She rested her elbows on her knees and covered her face with her hands. "Only, you didn't tell her about the kiss, did you?"

He put a hand to her back and rubbed gently. "I didn't have to. She told me she'd fallen in love in Galveston and couldn't marry me."

"I'm sorry." She dropped her hands to her lap and

made herself look at him. "Chelsea implied we were fooling around while Caroline was gone."

"It'll all be forgotten by tomorrow," he said. "Don't worry about it. Have you had anything for lunch besides those chocolates?"

"No. I wasn't hungry," she explained illogically. "I just *needed* chocolate."

"Then all you have in your stomach is sugar and caffeine." He grinned. "In your state of mind, you're a danger to yourself and society. Let me take you to lunch."

She sighed dispiritedly. "Thanks, but that's not a good idea. It'll just add credence to Chelsea's story."

"And who is that a problem for?"

"No one, I suppose, but you'll probably just use the time to lobby me to change my mind." She really wanted to go to lunch with him. She'd love to spend time in his company before he went back to Dallas, but it wasn't wise. And she was supposed to be.

"No, I won't," he said seriously. "You were very clear about how you felt yesterday, and I'll respect that."

She felt another small twinge of disappointment. She had to stick to her decision, but a little more reluctance on his part to comply would have been welcome, a little expression of sadness appreciated.

"I'm grateful for that," she lied.

"You're welcome. You want to go to Austin Eats for your usual salad?"

She didn't. She wanted something greasy and full of calories. "Do you like Tex-Mex?"

"Sure."

"Then let's go. There's a great place just a couple of blocks away."

Anna wasn't sure if it was the spice of the meal or the freedom of knowing that Austin had accepted her decision about their relationship and was no longer a threat to her peace of mind, but after their lunch she felt livelier than she had all day.

"So, I presume there'll be no knights in armor at the old folks' wedding?" Austin said as they walked toward her office. The light turned red when they were halfway across the crosswalk, and Austin caught her hand and ran the rest of the way.

She followed him breathlessly, then collided with him on the opposite curb when he stopped. She felt his warmth, his solid strength, and her good humor was dented just a little by the knowledge that he wasn't meant for her.

But she left her hand companionably in his as they continued to walk.

"No armor, no ivy arches, no horses." She turned to him questioningly. "Do you have to send your horses to Las Vegas for Caroline's wedding?"

He shook his head. "She's wisely decided to forgo the horses. But I understand you're shipping the armor?"

"Right. Pack and Ship's coming tomorrow to pack them up for me and take them away. I'm going to miss them. I've been bouncing ideas off them, telling them my secrets."

"You have secrets?" he asked in surprise. "I thought you were honest to a fault. Except where I'm concerned, of course."

HE FELT the instant tension in the hand he held. So there *was* a secret. He pretended not to notice.

She scolded him with a glance. "I've been perfectly honest with you from the beginning, if you recall. I told you what I thought about your marrying Caroline for a baby."

"Yes, you did." But he knew he wasn't getting the truth about why Anna wouldn't marry him. She'd told him she didn't want another baby, and with her only child ten years old, that could very well be true.

But he didn't think so. He couldn't come up with anything to back up the hunch, but it was strong anyway. He'd known her barely a week, but he knew her as well as he knew himself.

That wasn't to say he understood her, but he felt a connection that went beyond understanding, like some cosmic tie born when God mapped out destinies.

Anna was his woman.

"Are you feeling all right today?" she asked, stopping them in the middle of the sidewalk to look at him in puzzlement.

Good. His psychology was working.

"What do you mean?" he asked innocently.

"You're always arguing with me," she said. "But today you're not. You're agreeing with me or letting an argument slide."

He started walking again, drawing her with him with a casual shrug he was far from feeling.

"That's because it's important to get your point across," he explained, "if you're going to share a future with a woman. She has to know where you stand. But if you're not going to stay together it's pointless to argue, isn't it?"

He caught the same look of sad disappointment he'd seen in her eyes before. It caused him pain, but it encouraged him, also.

"I suppose," she said. She gave him a small grin that was amusedly wistful. "But it feels unnatural."

"We could find something unimportant to argue about," he suggested, stopping at a light. "Though I'm a capitalist, I'm a screaming liberal at heart. What about you? Conservative?"

She stopped beside him, shaking her head. "No. Sorry. Liberal, too."

"How do you feel about jazz?"

"Hate it."

"Darn. Me, too. Horror movies?"

"Love them."

"So do I. I know! Football."

"No opinion."

"Oh. Anchovies on pizza?"

"Don't like them."

"Me neither." They slowed their pace as they approached the building that housed her office.

"Well, that didn't work," he said. "I guess we'd have to be married to find something unimportant to fight about."

"So, this is goodbye, then," she said, trying to sound casual. But he knew better. She didn't want it to be the end of their brief and eventful relationship.

So why was she doing this?

Damned if he knew.

"You're supposed to pick me up for Will's Fathers

and Careers Day on Friday," he said. "Then I guess, it's goodbye."

They reached her building, and he opened the door for her.

"But this is the last time we'll be alone," she said as they walked to the elevator at the other end of the small lobby. Her voice was throaty and strained.

He wanted to shake her and make her tell him what the secret was, but he knew it was smarter to bide his time. He pressed the up button, and the elevator doors parted instantly on an empty car. They walked in.

"And I wanted to tell you," she said, pushing the button to her floor, "that I'm sorry you aren't getting your baby."

He wasn't sure how far to push this, but he'd never been cautious—in business or in life.

"If you won't give me one out of love," he said, pushing all the way, "I'll find someone who'll do it for other reasons. And who knows? Love grows in unexpected places."

She was pale when they reached her floor. He walked her to her office door.

He was feeling triumphant when she turned to him and looped her arms around his neck. He saw the kiss in her eyes even before she stood on tiptoe to reach him.

Her eyes were filled with love for him, and behind that, a pain that pleated her forehead. Her warm red lips parted as messages he couldn't interpret crossed her face. Affection and grief were curiously intermingled, and he was more confused than ever.

Then she framed his face in her hands and lowered it to hers, rising on tiptoe to meet his mouth.

It was the kiss every man wants from a woman when he finally understands what love is all about. It wasn't sex or coquetry or anything to do with power, though she'd definitely taken the initiative.

This was soul-baring love, the unselfish sharing of everything she felt. Her fingertips were tender, her lips artful and ardent, her arms around him a little desperate as she held him one last, protracted moment.

Then she dropped them and took a step back. Tears pooled in her bottom lids.

"Bye, Austin," she whispered.

It required every particle of character he possessed to stop himself from throwing her on the fainting couch and keeping her there until she told him the truth. Instead, summoning the self-control he was known for, he made himself say goodbye and walk away.

HE PACED the hotel suite all afternoon, praying that she would call, tell him she'd reconsidered, that she wanted to talk, that she couldn't live without him, after all.

But it was five o'clock and he hadn't heard a word from her. She and Will would be leaving the office, going down to Austin Eats for dinner or home to Rojalia's cooking.

He went to the window and looked down on the thickening traffic. The sun was low, its light frail, the whole landscape gray and somehow hostile. He noticed the silence of his room and wondered how he could possibly pick up the threads of his life and go on in the same old way.

He had to, of course. The livelihoods of too many people depended on it. But it wouldn't be fun anymore.

The telephone rang. He'd waited for the sound for so long that he turned to stare at the instrument, wondering if his mind had created the ring or if it had truly happened.

Then it happened again.

"Austin Cahill," he said calmly into the receiver.

"Hi, Austin!" It was Will. "Mom and I are going to see an old horror movie at the Strand! She said I could take a friend, and I picked you."

Austin smiled, applauding the woman's style. She *didn't* want to say goodbye, but she could blame this brief reunion on her son. Clever.

But he was clever, too. More time spent with her meant more opportunity to wear her down.

"Great," he said. "Where'll I meet you?"

"We'll pick you up in ten minutes. The movie's at six, then Mom says Rojalia left us lots of cold chicken and salad."

A chance to go home with her. Excellent.

"I'll be waiting downstairs," he said.

The Strand was showing *The House of Wax*. Anna, Austin and Will found seats halfway back, and Anna sat between them with the jumbo bucket of popcorn.

Will's eyes were glued to the screen as he ate popcorn to the tempo of the suspenseful music. He left several times to go to the lobby for more treats, but always returned at a run to resume his place and stare in fascinated horror at the movie screen.

Anna was also lost in the story of the man who populated a lifelike wax museum with the bodies of those he killed.

Vincent Price was at his evil best, a host of beautiful young women supporting him and becoming his hapless victims. When he finally trapped the heroine and prepared to lower her into a vat of boiling wax, Will climbed over their feet and fell into the chair beside Austin.

"She isn't gonna die, is she?" he asked in a loud whisper, sinking down in his seat.

"No," Austin whispered back.

"Have you seen this before?"

"No."

"Then how do you know?"

Anna shushed them, her eyes on the action.

Austin leaned over the boy to say quietly, "Because the hero and the heroine always survive. It's the code of the old B movie."

Just as Austin spoke the words, rescue arrived and the heroine was saved.

Will sagged against Austin in relief. "You were right!" he said in amazement. "Her boyfriend came along at the last minute and saved her!"

The credits rolled and the theater lights went on.

"That's a hero's job," Austin said.

"I wonder why she went in that dark room to begin with?" Will asked.

"You got me. I'd have run in the other direction, myself."

"What if you knew that a beautiful lady was in there?"

"I'd still be running."

Will studied him closely, unable to determine if he was telling the truth or teasing.

"What if the woman was Mom?"

Smart child. "Then I'd have risked everything without a second thought," he replied. "And I'd have done the same if you'd been in there."

Will seemed to like that assurance. He smiled widely and beamed at his mother. "Did you hear that? He'd have saved us."

"Good." Finally free of the movie's spell, Anna looked from Will to Austin with that sweet, but carefully removed, look in her eyes. "We have his cell phone number. The next time we're about to be tipped into a vat of wax, we'll call him. Ready to go?"

Austin and Will walked out together, following Anna.

"I know she likes you," Will said to Austin. "How come she won't say so? How come sometimes she acts like she *doesn't?*"

"I can't say for sure," Austin told him as they followed her to the car parked half a block away. "But when you admit you care about somebody, it's a little dangerous. Sort of like being tossed into a vat of wax."

"But then they'd love you back. How is that bad?"

"Sometimes when you haven't been loved very much, you're afraid you don't know how, or that you just can't do it. I used to feel that way."

Will looked up at him interestedly. "What changed your mind?"

"Actually, your mother did." Austin smiled over the complexities of love and romance. "But it's possible I can't do the same for her. And you can't force someone to feel love. They do or they don't."

Will frowned. "What if she does feel it, but just can't say it?"

"I think if you feel it," Austin said, "there comes a point where you *have* to say it. At least, that's the theory I'm working on."

"All right!" Will smiled conspiratorially. "Then good luck, Austin. Oh, and did anybody buy the pet shops yet?"

"Not yet."

"Are you thinking about the puppies?"

ANNA WASN'T SURE what had happened, but when she unlocked the car doors and walked around to the driver's side, she saw her companions trailing behind her, Will dangling upside down from Austin's right arm and laughing hysterically.

CHAPTER ELEVEN

AUSTIN AND WILL joked and sparred through a casual dinner of cold leftovers and salad at the dining room table.

Will went to the refrigerator for pizza left from the previous day, then for the fudge brownies Rojalia had made for him.

"Where are you putting all that?" Austin asked. "You had a jumbo popcorn, licorice and a giant box of Dots at the movie."

Will shrugged and kept eating. "Just always hungry. Want another brownie?"

Her son's delight in Austin's attention made Anna realize that although Will was well adjusted and happy, having a man around on a regular basis would benefit him a great deal. His uncles spent as much time with him as they could, but Will needed someone for whom he was all-important. Someone besides her.

And Austin seemed to like Will's company. Anna saw his enjoyment of her son's intelligence and intuitive observations, his amusement at Will's sharp sense of humor. If only time could be turned back.

But that was a futile hope. She had to deal with the here and now. And that was why she'd hit upon the plan to let Will invite him to spend the evening with them. If she could muster the guts and the eloquence, she would tell him why she couldn't marry him. She just couldn't say goodbye without explaining.

Will finally excused himself to do homework.

Anna pretended heart failure.

Looking around her at Austin, Will rolled his eyes. "You'd think I never did it."

"You do do it," she conceded, carrying plates into the kitchen. "But usually after I've resorted to threats."

He grinned winningly. "Maybe I'm maturing."

She kissed his forehead. "Don't you dare. You're growing up fast enough already. Pretty soon you'll leave me for college, then you'll come home for Christmas with a cheerleader, then you'll graduate and move to New York to work for some big stockbroker and all I'll ever get is pictures of the grandkids."

Will put a hand on her arm. "Mom. Chill. I'm in the sixth grade."

"I know." She kissed him again and turned him toward the stairs. "Call me when you're ready to go to sleep."

"Right." But instead of heading for the stairs, he turned to the table where Austin was gathering bowls. He held out his hand.

Austin put the bowls down and shook it. "Good night, Will. Study hard. When you graduate, you can come work for me, and you'll be close enough that your mom can see the grandkids and not just their pictures."

Will smiled broadly. "Wouldn't that be cool? I could be your right-hand man!"

"Yes, you could."

"What would you pay me?"

Anna saw Austin bite back a smile. "Generously," he replied. "With bonuses for moneymaking or money-saving ideas."

"Hey. I can do that. Are you ready for Fathers and Careers Day?"

"Almost. My staff's helping me with a presentation."

Will remained one more moment that might have been awkward had her son been less candid. "Would you be embarrassed if I hugged you?" he asked Austin.

Austin shook his head. "Would you?"

"No."

"Then..."

Austin opened his arms, and Will hugged him soundly. "See you in the morning when Mom picks you up."

"Right."

Glowing with happiness, Will ran upstairs.

Austin picked up the bowls again and carried them into the kitchen, where Anna loaded the dishwasher. "That boy is smarter and more fun to be with than most adults I know. Plastic wrap or something to cover these in the refrigerator?"

"The drawer right in front of you," she said. Then she gave him a big smile to hide her nervousness. "He gets that from me, you know."

He measured out a length of wrap across the width

of the bowl of pasta salad, then tore it off. Or tried to. It resisted his effort, stretched instead of tore, and when he tried to tear it from the other end, it bunched together and stuck to itself.

"How many CEOs does it take to tear a length of plastic wrap?" he joked, fighting with it.

She laughed and went to help. "With the help of a wedding planner," she said, "only one." She discarded the ruined piece, then tore off a new one and fitted it onto the bowl. "Actually, it's nice to know there's something you can't do."

He frowned at her in pretended displeasure. "So you have to know my imperfections to be comfortable with me?"

"No," she replied without thinking. "I've always been comfortable with you."

That was an admission she hadn't intended to make, but it was too late now. He looked at her in mild perplexity, a hand on the counter as he watched her work.

"You disapproved of my reason for asking Caroline to marry me."

"I did, but that's different. I know some men who are supposed to be paragons of virtue and compassion, and something about them makes me uncomfortable. But you never have. Maybe because Will likes you. He's always been a good judge of character."

She was chattering. Tension bounced off the cupboards as he shifted position to take the bowls from her and put them in the refrigerator. She breathed a sigh of relief when he went to the table for the butter dish and the breadbasket. Then he was back and it started all over again.

She put a bottle of brandy on a tray with two snifters and pointed him to the living room. "Why don't you pour these and I'll be along as soon as I'm finished in here."

"Let me help."

She shooed him away. "I'm almost finished."

He walked away with the tray and she leaned against the counter and closed her eyes, putting a hand to her pounding heart.

"Where was all this excitement and emotion," she whispered to herself, "when you were a girl? John never made you feel like this, and you sincerely thought you had a future with him. You know there isn't a chance for you and Austin, and yet you're on the brink of an old-fashioned swoon. It's not only illogical, but stupid."

Okay. Armed with that stern talking-to, she started the dishwasher, wiped off the counters one more time to give herself a few extra seconds, then squared her shoulders and walked into the living room.

Austin had built a fire that was just beginning to burn through the expertly placed teepee of logs. Brandy pooled in two glasses on the coffee table and picked up the fire's glow.

"CEO *and* Boy Scout?" she teased nervously.

He must have caught the little break in her voice because he pushed up on his knees and stood in one graceful motion, his eyes studying hers, looking for an explanation.

She wanted to turn away so he couldn't read anything in her expression until she could make herself tell him, but his gaze felt suddenly like a tractor beam and she couldn't look away.

"I don't understand, Anna," he said frankly.

"I know you don't." She sighed. "I have to explain."

"I wish you would."

She started for the sofa, determined to make a clean breast of the situation once and for all, when Will called.

"Okay, Mom!" he shouted from his room. "And can Austin come, too?"

She felt absurdly grateful for the reprieve, but tried to pretend otherwise. "Already?" she asked. "It's only been twenty minutes. I thought you had homework."

"I'm a smart kid," he shouted, laughter in his voice. "I'm done!"

Giddy with relief, she laughed.

"Ever done a tucking in before?" she asked Austin.

He accepted the interruption with a smile. "Never."

"It's one of the perks of parenthood. Come on. You'll have to know how to do this for...for when you have your baby."

"Okay. Lead on."

WILL LAY propped up against his pillows, the blankets pulled to his waist in a single bed in a handsomely furnished child's room decorated with posters of everyone Austin knew. He was a little startled to find his own face there in an antiabuse promotion he'd taken part in.

Will grinned as Austin followed Anna to the side of his bed.

Austin felt suddenly as though he'd just awakened and found himself at home after a long, dark night. As though he'd finally, however accidentally, blundered into his *real* life.

This was where he belonged. Not in the mansion outside Dallas, but here, with a grinning child and a dark-eyed woman who watched him with love in her eyes. He discounted her refusal to marry him and the strange, wistful expression she sometimes wore when she thought he wasn't watching.

Something snapped into place inside him. A deal made with himself. He wasn't leaving. And she wasn't getting away, no matter how hard she tried or how difficult she made it for him.

Without warning, Anna tickled Will unmercifully until he squealed and howled and doubled up to fend her off.

"First you torture them," she said to Austin as though giving him instructions. She pulled the covers to Will's chin. "Then they're very cooperative when you tuck them in."

"I see."

She worked the blankets in along the length of him, then under his feet. "And you tuck really tightly so they can't get out of bed and raid the refrigerator."

"Got it."

"Then you ask them if they need a glass of water, otherwise they'll call you for it when you're downstairs again and they're too well tucked in to get it themselves.''

"Hmm."

"Do you want a glass of water, Will?" she asked.

"Yes, please," he said.

She excused herself to Austin. "Be right back."

When she left the room, headed for the bathroom across the hall, Will sat up, grabbed Austin's wrist and pulled him down beside him. "How's it going?" he demanded, eyes wide.

"Well...it's only been twenty—"

"So she hasn't said it yet," Will interrupted.

"No."

"But you think you can make her?"

"I'm going to do my best."

"Okay. I'm going right to sleep so you'll have privacy. And I won't call for water or anything."

"Thank you," Austin replied seriously. "That's much appreciated."

"Here she comes!" Will whispered urgently. "Pretend you're tucking me in!"

Anna handed Will the glass of water.

Austin smiled at her as he rearranged the blankets. "He...moved to check his alarm clock. I was testing my skills."

Will took a long gulp, then handed back the water with a deep breath. "I think he's got the hang of it, Mom."

"Good," Anna said. "Anything else you need?"

"Nope. Good night, you guys."

Anna leaned over Will and kissed his cheek. "You kiss them," she said to Austin when she straightened.

"It's the only time they let you do it, so you take advantage of it. Go ahead. Even fathers, uncles, friends can do it."

Austin leaned over Will to kiss his cheek. Will hugged Austin and whispered quietly, "Good luck!"

Anna turned off the light as Austin straightened, and they walked out of the room, leaving the door slightly ajar. "You never close the door all the way," she whispered loud enough for Will to hear, "because you spy on them all the time. It's the only way."

"Makes sense to me."

As Austin followed Anna down the stairs, he felt life coursing through his body in a way he'd never experienced before. This was love, he knew. This was what it felt like to care so much about a woman that her essence ran in your blood.

The fire burned brightly in the fireplace, their untouched snifters of brandy jeweled in its glow.

She went to the fire instead of the sofa, as though drawn to the flames and their warmth. She rubbed her arms as she stared into it.

He lifted her snifter off the coffee table, turning it in his hands to warm it as he went to stand beside her.

OKAY, THIS'LL BE EASY, Anna told herself. *Just let the truth come out, he'll tell you it's been nice, and then he'll leave. It'll be hell, but this push and pull between what you want and what you can realistically have will be over. And both of you can get on with your lives. Now, be a woman. Look into his eyes and tell him what he has to know.*

Anna was used to talking herself into things; she did it all the time. Her mother had trained all her children to be people of character and moral strength, but there were times when there were options far more appealing than the high road. And this was one of them.

She squared her shoulders, drew a breath and turned to Austin, who'd come to stand beside her in front of the fire.

And then she knew that listening to herself had been a mistake. Looking him in the eye only served to remind her how very special he was and how much she'd come to love him.

She opened her mouth to speak, but he offered her a brandy glass warmed in his hands, his eyes smiling and indulgent, as though he accepted her oddly ambivalent behavior even when he couldn't understand it. She knew that was more generous than she could ever be.

He smiled gently and reached out to smooth her hair. "You were starting to tell me something," he reminded her, "when Will called you."

Caught in the snare of his warmth and the seduction of his acceptance, she felt the truth rise out of her as though from a fountain.

"I love you, Austin," she said with absolute sincerity. "I love you so much."

It wasn't the truth she'd originally intended to share, but it was the reality that controlled everything at the moment, and there was no holding it back. She said it again and again. "I love you. I love you."

His eyes reflected surprise for one instant, then he

reclaimed the brandy, placed it on the table and took her into his arms.

She laughed, discovering a certain ecstasy in the freedom earned by the admission. It occurred to her that the words were binding, an imprisonment of sorts, but she didn't feel that way at all. The emotions she'd banked for so long ignited and burned away all her fears.

He raised an eyebrow, his eyes staring into hers, a smile widening in response to her laughter. "You do know what you're doing?" he asked. "You haven't started on the brandy without me?"

She laughed again, bringing his face down for a kiss, a growing need to touch him swelling inside her. "I'm quite sober. It's the sanest statement I've ever made."

And that seemed to be all he wanted to know. He took the throw from the back of the sofa, placed it close to the fire, then knelt on it and drew her down beside him.

"It's been a long…" She began to speak as he unfastened the buttons on her sweater. "I mean, I haven't—"

He silenced her with a kiss as he finished the task and eased the sweater off her shoulders.

"Since Will was born!" she said urgently when he finally freed her lips, her mind registering in mild panic just how long that had been.

He grinned and reached around her for the hooks on her bra. "All that passion saved up," he said. "That's good, not bad."

He pulled the bra straps off her arms and tossed

the lace aside, reacting with flattering wonder as he took her full breasts gently into his hands.

Sensation rippled through her, and she looped her arms around his neck, marveling that such feelings could still be called up after lying dormant for ten years.

He held her close. His wool sweater was pleasantly rough against the tips of her breasts, his fingertips deliciously tender in contrast as he stroked her back and shoulders.

She wedged a small space between them to tug his shirt out of his pants, and he unbuttoned and unzipped her slacks.

When she'd freed him of his sweater and shirt, she leaned into him, loving the sensation of his warmth and muscle against her softness.

He expelled a broken breath. "I can't tell you," he said, "how many times I've imagined this."

"Me, too," she whispered. "Only it's even...more wonderful."

"Yes. Destiny."

She looked at him, smiling ruefully. "I wonder why destiny lets you screw up before you find it."

"To make sure you really want it, maybe?" He took a throw pillow off the sofa, tossed it onto the afghan, then urged her to lie back. In several efficient movements, he rid her of shoes and socks, slacks and panties, then shed his clothes.

AUSTIN COULDN'T quite believe this was happening, but he wasn't pausing to question. Maybe he should be allowing for her second thoughts, but she was smiling with her lips *and* with her eyes, and she lifted her arms to welcome him as he settled beside her. Her hands moved over him eagerly. She seemed to be very single-minded.

And he was definitely of the same mind.

She was silk and satin under his hands, passion alive and needing only his exploratory touch to make it flame.

She seemed surprised by her shallow breaths, by her rapid readiness for him. She said his name on a startled note and tried to pull him to her, but he was finding his own pleasure in how new it all seemed to her.

For a man for whom sex had ceased to mean anything significant, it was an education and a delight.

ANNA HAD NEVER felt this. In the beginning she'd had the occasional pleasure with John, but for the most part it had been laborious, and over before she'd enjoyed it.

But this was... There were no words for it. And thinking required that she divert part of her attention from feeling, and what she was feeling suddenly demanded her complete focus.

Pleasure broadsided her, and she took it greedily, absorbing the fullness of its tender assault. Every toe and every fingertip pulsed with it.

Then, ashamed that she'd focused on herself, she wrapped her arms around Austin and gave his body all the careful attention he'd given hers, exploring with her lips and fingertips.

"But I wasn't finished—" he began.

She silenced him with a carefully placed touch, and he groaned, his argument lost. Inspired by that success, she pinned him to the blanket and strummed and stroked him from collarbone to knee until he caught her by the shoulders and turned them so that he was uppermost. He kissed her fiercely and then he entered her with a smooth power that brought her pleasure in an instant.

Every little corner of her body came alive, and the heart that had lived quietly for so long pounded its message of life and love.

She wrapped her legs around his waist, and her body tightened on him until they gasped together in shared fulfillment.

AS AUSTIN DREW ANNA against his side, he wondered what had ever seemed so fulfilling about making money. This was fulfillment—a man's body subdued by the gentle powers of his woman, then brought to the absolute pinnacle of pleasure by her artful hands.

Then another thought struck him. Soon Anna would have his baby. Perhaps not from this encounter, but from the next, or the one after that. And that doubled, tripled the pleasure.

That daydream was disturbed by the vague memory of Anna telling him she didn't want more children. But then she had been unable to believe in him as a lover or a husband. Tonight she'd made it clear that she trusted him, believed in him.

He kissed the top of her head and rubbed lovingly from her shoulder to her elbow as she clutched his waist.

"I love you," he said.

She held him more tightly and whispered against his chin. "I love you, too."

"Good. Then we're agreed." He knew he was pushing it, but after knowing her, in the personal *and* in the biblical sense, there was no way he could live without her. "We're getting married."

After her enthusiastic response to him and the creative initiative she'd taken on her own, he expected a clear affirmative.

When he heard nothing, he experienced a niggle of concern. When he felt her tears on his throat, dread reared its ugly head.

ANNA CONTINUED to hold him, even when she felt tension invade his body, felt it tighten in the arm around her.

It was all her fault, but it had been an innocent mistake. She'd intended to tell him one truth, but her love for him had forced out another. And now she had to face one of life's major dirty tricks—though the world turned on truth, it was entirely possible to find two truths that were not compatible.

"What is it?" His voice came out of the firelight, quiet and, to her ears at least, ominous.

She kissed his throat. "I love you, Austin," she said, her voice thick with emotion. "That is God's honest truth." She pushed herself to a sitting position beside him and said grimly, "But it isn't the truth I'd originally intended to tell you."

She reached for her sweater and pulled it on, feeling naked and vulnerable. Now that she really understood what she was about to lose, pleasure faded and pain took hold. She knew, though, that she would never forget what it was like to make love with him. Never.

When she handed him his sweater, he sat up, too, frowning. He pulled it on. "You're not going to confess a past, are you?" he asked, his head emerging from the neckhole. "Because I don't give a rip. I'm the man who bargained with a woman to get a baby, remember?"

Her suddenly sorrowful gaze tore right into him. What, he wondered grimly, could make her look like that?

She sorted and distributed underthings.

"Wait," he said, and caught her wrist to stop her. "We're not going to talk about this—whatever it is— while pulling on underwear."

He yanked the throw out from under him and placed it over their laps. They sat cross-legged, face to face. "What? What is it?"

Tears smarted in her eyes and stung her throat. It was not self-pity, but acute frustration over her powerlessness to change the situation. She fought desperately against letting the tears fall. "It's the baby," she said.

He looked confused. "You mean...the deal I made with Caroline?"

She shook her head, and a tear fell anyway. "I mean the deal you *can't* make with me."

"I know you said you didn't want another baby," he began, studying her closely, "but I thought that was because you didn't trust me then. We just made love. Don't you trust me now?''

She opened her mouth to answer, but her throat was so tight, the words wouldn't come.

"I'd never shortchange Will in preference to our baby," he went on, "if that's what you're worried about.''

Though her lips quivered, she fought against it and said firmly, "I know that. And it was never that I didn't want another baby. It's just easier to tell yourself you don't want one when you can't have one.''

"Can't have one," he repeated warily.

She made herself meet his eyes, and like the last time she did that, all she saw in him, all she thought about was love. And then she began to cry because it was so sad.

"Can't have one!" she said, weeping. "I had a complete hysterectomy three years ago.''

He stared at her, clearly speechless.

"I had a kidney infection," she heard herself explain, as though that would help make the truth more palatable. "I had scarring and pain..." She drew a breath and emitted a loud sob. "There was no alternative. So...that's that.''

IT TOOK A MOMENT for the significance of the words to penetrate his surprise, for him to reshape his plans for the future. The moment he grasped it, he felt consumed with anger, though he wasn't entirely sure where to direct it. Certainly not at Anna, sobbing into her hands over something that was obviously causing her such grief.

Then where? At himself, for wanting what everyone else found with relative ease? At the fates, who'd given him this desire for a child, found him the perfect woman with whom to have it, then placed this insurmountable obstacle in their way?

He couldn't decide. He just knew he felt it. And he had to move.

He pulled on his clothes while Anna wept, then he paced, unaccustomed to a problem he couldn't solve.

"Why didn't you tell me?" It seemed a pertinent question. Not necessarily sensitive at the moment, but pertinent.

She was wiping her face with the ends of the throw. "Because I didn't think I'd ever have to," she explained defensively. "I couldn't believe anything would come of a relationship between us, then when it did, it was just easier to make you believe I didn't want it to happen than to have to explain why." She gave him a condemning look. "Only you're so damned stubborn."

"Well, pardon me," he said a little loudly, "for meaning it when I say I love you."

"Well, pardon me," she snapped, slipping into her panties under the concealment of the blanket, "for wanting to protect you from what I knew you couldn't deal with!"

Then she tossed the throw aside and pulled on her slacks.

She hopped on one foot to slip on the second pant leg and almost lost her balance. Austin reached out to steady her and earned a glare for his trouble.

"I like to decide for myself what I can and can't deal with!" he growled at her.

"Do you want a baby?"

"Yes, damn it!"

"Then you can't deal with me because I can never, ever give you one! There are no fertility tricks that will work on me."

Austin was trying desperately to get a grip on this situation. Making love to Anna had been a life-altering experience, and only moments ago he'd envisioned their future together spreading before them like a gold ribbon.

The last few minutes of their conversation, however, had bombed every bit of it, and he wanted to move carefully over the terrain.

"First of all," he said reasonably, "let's stop shouting."

She yanked the blanket off the floor and folded it in four. "If you'd listen to me," she said grimly, "I wouldn't have to shout."

"I'm listening," he replied patiently. "I heard you. And I can usually think quickly, but when I'm surprised, it takes a little more time."

Tossing the blanket at the sofa, she went to the fireplace, took the poker and knocked the logs apart to squelch the fire.

"That's my fault," she said. The last flames leaped up, highlighting her hair and the porcelain of her face. "I intended to tell you tonight so that we could talk about it sensibly and see if you...still wanted...a relationship. But I turned to you to look into your eyes and tell you the truth and..." Her voice caught, and she shook her head. "But you have this way of...of looking at me that makes me forget all the reasonable and responsible parts of my life and think only about..."

She replaced the poker with a clang and drew a breath, folding her arms and leaning against the fireplace.

"I know it wasn't fair to make love to you first and then tell you, but... I guess it was just self-indulgence. Or maybe I did really forget for a little while."

"I don't..." He began to try to explain that he really didn't care about the sequence of events, but she cut him off.

"The point is," she interrupted, going to the closet for his jacket, "that you want a baby and I can't give you one. So there's little point in hashing over everything." She held the jacket open for him to slip into. "You'd better go."

He suddenly had a direction for the anger. He yanked the coat from her and tossed it at a nearby chair. "That's it?" he demanded. "You make love with me as though we'll never see tomorrow, surprise me with stuff I should have known days ago, decide for me how I should react, then throw me out!"

"I'm trying to make it easy for you!"

"Well, thank you, but any more consideration for me on your part and I'll require psychiatric care!"

They glared at each other in the pulsing silence that followed that outburst, then a small voice said weakly, "Mom?"

Both turned to see Will in his pajamas, standing

halfway down the stairs. He was pale and big-eyed and rubbed a hand over his stomach. "I don't feel good."

Austin started for the stairs, but Anna pushed past him and ran up to put a diagnostic hand on her son's forehead. "No fever," she said calmly in a much quieter tone than she'd used with Austin. "I think you just ate too much today."

He nodded and made a face. "I think I'm gonna barf."

"Okay. Go up to the bathroom. I'm right behind you." She gave him a gentle shove and paused just long enough to look over the railing at Austin, her eyes both sad and angry. "Goodbye," she said with chilling conviction in the word.

Under normal circumstances, that was all he would have needed to remain planted where he stood until the mountains eroded, just to show her that she wasn't the final authority on everything.

But the circumstances were not normal, and as though he didn't already have sufficient proof of that, his jacket rang. He crossed to it and yanked out his cell phone.

"Well, *there* you are!" his mother's voice said in what sounded like exasperation. "I'm home from safari and I've tracked you to hell and back to find you. The hotel didn't know where you were, Caroline's sister told me she's gone to Vegas with another man. What's going on, Austin?"

Austin sank into the chair and put a hand over his eyes. If there was one complication he didn't need in his life right now, it was his mother.

"Where are you, Mom?" he asked.

"The airport," she replied.

"In New York?"

She laughed lightly. "Of course not, silly. In Austin. I missed you. Can you come and get me?"

He stifled a groan. "Sure," he said. "Get a cup of coffee and sit tight. I'll be right there."

"All right, darling. Wait till you see what I've brought you. Bye."

She hung up before he could ask what it was. Considering the bagpipes she'd brought him from Scotland and the life-size carving of a dancer from Bali, many arms included, he'd have liked to be prepared.

He ran up the stairs in search of Anna, but found the bathroom door closed. It sounded as though she had her hands full with Will.

He hesitated a moment, unwilling to leave without telling her, but then she'd said goodbye in a way that closed the door between them for good.

Or would have, if he wasn't as cussed as she was.

Still fuming, he ran downstairs and out to his car. It frosted him to let her think she'd had the final word on the issue, but Will was her priority right now. Austin had a few things to say on the subject, but he would have to choose his moment.

CHAPTER TWELVE

IN THE MIDDLE of crowded Robert Mueller Municipal Airport, Gloria Cahill, dressed in safari jacket over pocket pants and boots, presented her son with a four-foot tribal shield. And then a fierce hug and a kiss on each cheek.

"There," she said cheerfully. "Now you're protected against everything. A shield against your enemies and a hug and kisses to blunt the pain your friends can sometimes inflict." She tucked her arm in his as they headed for the baggage claim area. Her look into his eyes was a mother's careful study. "I'm sorry about Caroline."

"Don't be," he said, patting her hand on his arm. "She's happier than I've ever seen her. She's really in love."

She caught his fingers with her thumb. "But where does that leave you?"

"Actually," he admitted, because she would see it eventually anyway, "I'm in love, too."

"With...Caroline?"

"No. Watch it, Mom. That cart's going to run you over."

She obliged him by stepping aside, then waited until they'd reached baggage claim to resume their conversation. "With whom, then?"

He grinned, knowing how the details would sound. "With the woman who was planning our wedding."

"Austin!" she gasped, half shocked, half amused. "You're kidding!"

"I'm not."

"Well…how did you let that happen?"

"I didn't *let* it happen," he said, positioning her by a post a short distance from the baggage carousel. "It happened to me. And to her."

Her eyes lit up. "You mean she loves you, too?"

"Yes."

Her smile lasted another moment, then she studied him feature by feature and finally asked bluntly, "Then why are you in pain?"

He groaned and handed her his jacket. "Wait here. Just the usual three bags?"

She had a pink and gray tapestry set that he'd checked and picked up for her at every airport on the eastern seaboard and the Gulf of Mexico.

"And a spear!" she called after him.

He stopped in his tracks and turned to her. "A spear?"

She shrugged. "To go with the shield."

Of course.

He explained about Anna and Will on the drive to the hotel, then on the elevator to his suite. A bellman followed them with the cart that bore Gloria's luggage and the shield and spear. Tactfully, he pretended not to notice anything out of the ordinary.

"And her son's a stock market genius at ten years old?" she asked as he unlocked the door.

Austin smiled as he thought about Will. "He's the cutest kid. Scary smart, but deep down just a lovable kid."

She patted his cheek as she preceded him into the suite. "You were like that. Well. Isn't this lovely? I understand your office is wondering when you're coming home."

"Into the bedroom, please," Austin told the bellman.

The young man complied, Austin tipped him, Gloria thanked him sweetly, then held the suite door open for him.

He was charmed.

Austin wondered, not for the first time, what his mother might have accomplished as a young woman had circumstances been different. She had a natural gift for handling people.

"Soon." He led her to the bedroom the maid had already cleaned. "I have to get Anna straightened out first. You can have this room. I'll take the sofa."

His mother stood at the foot of the bed while he gathered the few things he'd left on the bedside table.

"Darling," she said quietly. "Straightening Anna out is not the right attitude if you're hoping to make her see things your way."

"She has attitude problems of her own." He walked into the living area with his belongings and dropped them onto a well-equipped desk placed in front of a window that looked onto Lake Austin. "It just levels out the playing field."

"It's not a game, Austin."

"I know what it is, Mother."

"It's your happiness. And hers. And that scary smart little boy's."

She put her hands on his arms and pushed until she'd backed him onto the sofa. Then she sat beside him, just as she had when he'd been eight and she'd told him his father wasn't coming back.

He felt the same edgy anger now that he'd felt then.

"I think you should look at this from her perspective," she said. "Try to put yourself in her place. I know that's trite advice, but it's the only way compromise is ever reached."

"Her perspective," he began, forcing himself to deal patiently with his meddlesome mother. She meant well, but in one of her I-know-how-to-fix-it-for-you moods, she made him crazy. "Her perspective," he repeated, "is that we can't have a relationship. And that I have no plans to compromise."

"You'll have to make her think that's what you're doing," she insisted, "or she won't even listen. And I think you should let a day or two pass so that you've calmed down, and she's not only willing to listen but eager for the sound of your voice."

He thought that over for a moment and decided he could grant her that one. It made good sense. But staying away from Anna for several days would be not only difficult, but, at the moment, impossible. He had a date to speak to Will's class the day after tomorrow.

He explained that to his mother.

"Well, that'll work," she said. "Just don't bring

up the issue unless she does, and my guess is she won't. The tension will be almost as good as absence."

He frowned at his mother. "I never realized you had such battlefield savvy."

She smiled sweetly. "I was a single mother. We learn skills men can't even imagine."

"And you use them on us," he accused with a grin.

"Of course. You're the opponent."

He shook his head in horrified disbelief. "Mom! You're the one who taught me to respect women as my equals."

"I did," she conceded. "And you'll note that I said men and women are opponents, not enemies. You can't blame me for that. Nature so ordained it. It doesn't mean we'll never come together, it just means we'll almost always approach a common ground from opposite directions, that's all. And only those who aren't afraid to challenge what they think they know, and stand in the other person's shoes, can ever find happiness with someone else. That's what your father couldn't do."

He studied the cheerful serenity of her expression and the patina of maturity she wore like an ermine wrap and brought her hand to his lips. "I'm sorry your life's been such a struggle," he said. He thought that often but seldom voiced it.

Her eyes widened in genuine surprise. "All I ever wanted out of my life was for you to grow up strong and happy and with a personally satisfying level of success." She emitted a youthful giggle. "I think we can consider ourselves overachievers."

THERE WERE Maitlands and Maitland mates everywhere. Anna's brothers and sisters and friends and co-workers filled the living room and dining room and sat around the perimeters on folding chairs Anna had borrowed from the hospital's meeting room in order to celebrate her mother's birthday.

Gifts of every description surrounded Megan where she sat in the middle of the living room. Miles of discarded paper and ribbon were being carefully folded and saved by Beth, who intended to use them for crafts in the day care.

The mood was jocular, even hilarious, as everyone teased Megan about her age.

Anna, smile pasted on, wanted to die. She hadn't been prepared for how much it hurt to know that Austin was probably in his Dallas office by now, finding another hotel to buy or looking for sites on which to build new ones.

When she'd gone downstairs last night after finally getting Will back to bed, Austin had left. She'd known that would happen, she'd told herself as she doused the fire. That was the reaction she'd expected.

But it was hell to be right.

She slipped into the kitchen to put candles on the Black Forest birthday cake Rojalia had made.

It also hurt, she thought, to see so many of her family and friends in happy little pairs. And to know that she'd probably always remain the odd woman out.

She'd long ago accepted her infertility and understood deep down that it didn't diminish her as a woman. The adjustment had been easier because she had Will, but she'd never expected to want a baby with the desperation with which she wanted one now.

She would have loved to have given Austin what he wanted. He'd saved her son's life. It seemed only fair.

"Hey." R.J. appeared at her side and placed a fraternal arm around her shoulders. "What a party!" he said. "But you don't seem to be in a party mood. Do I have to beat up somebody for you?"

She sent him a sidelong grin and handed him a fireplace lighter. "Unless you think you can do damage to a bathroom scale. Would you light the candles, please?"

"Sure." He took the device from her. "I had to stomp our scale for Dana even before she was pregnant. I'm experienced." He allowed her to think for a moment that she'd sidetracked him, then he asked seriously, touching flame to candles, "Is it Cahill?"

"No." She said it firmly, briskly, hoping to convince him.

He turned to lean against the counter and look at her. "Then why were you and he discussing your kidney infection last night? And rather loudly?"

She dropped the cake server and stared at him in disbelief. This was a new record for the swift distribution of family gossip. "How could you possibly know that?"

"I asked Will why he looked pale. He said he got sick last night and had to interrupt your argument with Cahill. I asked him what you were arguing about." When she gave him a scolding look, he said, clearly unrepentant, "Looking out for you is my job.

He said that all he could hear was you shouting about your kidney infection. So, clever analyzer that I am, I've concluded that since Cahill was going to marry Caroline for a baby, and your surgery made it impossible for you to have one, you were arguing about the possibility of a future together."

She put a hand to her eyes. "I cannot believe what little privacy I have!"

He pulled her hand down. "Did he withdraw his proposal because you can't have children?" he demanded.

"What even makes you think he proposed?"

"Will said he and Cahill talked about it and Cahill told him he was going to."

She gasped again. Austin had discussed proposing to her with her son?

"So, what did he say when you told him?" R.J. asked. "I want the truth."

"He was surprised, of course."

"And angry?"

"Yes," she replied, "but the same way I'm angry about it. Because I'm powerless to change it."

He raised an eyebrow. "That sounds like a reasonable reaction."

"I know."

"Then what was the problem? What else did he say?"

"There wasn't much time to talk about it. Will came downstairs because he was sick, and by the time I got him to bed and went down again, Austin was gone. I heard his cell phone ring when I was taking Will upstairs."

R.J. looked puzzled. "Then you don't know what he thinks, except that he was surprised, which you could certainly allow him."

She nodded.

"Then what was the shouting that Will overheard?"

Anna was growing impatient with his questions and his unwillingness to see the problem. "I don't remember!" she said, raising her voice. Then recalling that there was a party going on beyond the door, she lowered it. "He wants a baby and I can't give him one. I didn't see what there was to discuss. I just...wanted him to leave."

"Before you'd talked about it?"

"What is there to talk about?"

"Well, *he* might have something to say about it."

"He's gone," she said, turning to her task. "I think that says it all."

R.J. took the cake server from her, put it on the counter and, lightly gripping her arms, gave her a shake. "Hey. Have you been single so long that you've forgotten a relationship involves two people with two opinions and two points of view? If he's gone, it's because you sent him away without finding out what he thought and felt. Come on, Anna. How fair is that?"

"He'll find someone," she said thinly, "with whom he can have a baby."

"That could be, but the decision should be his and not yours."

The kitchen door burst open, and Abby walked in.

Noting their grim expressions, she looked from one to the other in concern.

"Are you bullying her?" she asked R.J. while putting a hand on Anna's shoulder.

R.J. rolled his eyes. "Now, why would you presume I'm bullying her? Maybe she's picking on me."

Abby made a scornful sound. "Because you bully everybody. And Anna never picks on anyone." She smiled solicitously at her sister. "Would you like me to remove him from the kitchen?"

R.J. smirked. "You and what commando unit?"

"I don't need commandos," Abby said, holding both hands up and wiggling her fingers. "I happen to know that you're helpless when tickled on your left side." And she attacked.

He drew away from her, pressing his left arm to his side and threatening her with retribution.

Beth and Ellie came into the kitchen with offers to help, then noticing the commotion in the corner, hurried to lend Abby their support.

Anna smiled at her siblings' antics, grateful for their presence in her life. She had a solid, supportive family and wonderful friends. She might be lonely for a while, but she'd learned to cope with it before and she could do it again.

As the hilarity in the corner rose a decibel, she put plates on a tray and wondered who she was trying to kid. Her life would never be the same again, and she had to face it. She could carry on, but it wouldn't be fun anymore.

ANNA EXPECTED WILL to be beside himself with excitement the following morning as they drove to Austin's hotel to pick him up for Fathers and Careers Day. Will had put on his favorite shirt and jeans, but he was subdued.

"Do you have an introduction ready?" she asked, trying to draw him out.

He nodded from the seat beside her. "I got most of it from that *Forbes* article."

"Good. I knew you'd be well prepared."

"Sure."

He was silent for several blocks.

"I'm sorry," she said finally, "that this isn't working out the way you'd hoped. I know you wanted Austin to...to stay with us."

"It's okay," he said philosophically, though his pinched face didn't look at all as though he accepted it. "You told me it wouldn't happen. I just wanted it to, so I kept hoping." He studied her with a frown as she stopped at a light. "But I heard you say 'I love you.' A couple of times, even. So...I don't get what happened. Don't people who say 'I love you' get married?"

She swallowed a pointed lump in her throat. "Not always. Love is important, but sometimes other things are important, too. We talked about this, remember?"

"Yeah, but you didn't say *what* was more important. Is it because you can't have babies? 'Cause Austin was marrying Miss Lamont to have a baby, right?"

The light turned green, but she continued to study her son in surprise. They'd talked about the fact she couldn't have any more children only once, when she'd picked him up from R.J.'s, where he'd stayed while she had her surgery.

The car behind her honked, and she accelerated, splitting her attention between her astute son and the road.

"He has a right to want that." She was quick to explain. "Just like I wanted you very badly."

He nodded. "Like I want a dad. I mean, one who really cares about me. I understand."

Anna pulled up to the front entrance of the hotel, wondering how she could ever feel that her life lacked anything when she had such a child.

Then Austin, who'd been talking with the doorman, came to the car. He carried something large and square covered in dark plastic.

Anna popped the trunk, and he put it inside, then closed the trunk and climbed into the back of the car, filling it with his charm, his energy, the spicy fragrance of his aftershave.

"Good morning," he said politely, then gently cuffed the top of Will's head. "Hey, Will. Are we ready?"

Will looked over his shoulder at Austin with a small smile. "I'm ready. Are you?"

"You bet. I've got a video on DVD, a TV-DVD player combination and some handouts."

Will's smile widened despite his earlier grimness. "What are you going to hand out? Money?"

"Smart aleck," he replied. "You'll see. How are you feeling?"

Will nodded. "Good. I think I just ate too much. Isn't it weird that you can have too much cake and stuff, but you never get sick from carrots and spinach?''

In the rearview mirror, Anna caught Austin's nod. ''I know. The world's cockeyed.'' Austin met her gaze. ''How are you, Anna?''

''I'm fine, thank you,'' she replied in the same courteous, impersonal tone he used. She pulled out into the traffic and headed for the school.

And that was all they said to each other. Will and Austin talked about the dangers of day trading on home computers, virtually ignoring Anna.

When she finally pulled up in front of the school, Will unbuckled his seat belt and leaned over to kiss her cheek. ''Are you gonna pick us up? 'Cause Austin probably won't want to ride home on the school bus.''

Before she could reply, Austin said, ''I've got that handled. A car's coming for us. I'll bring him to your office, Anna.''

''Fine,'' she said with a smile in the mirror.

Austin slid out of the back and Anna popped the trunk so he could retrieve his equipment. He closed the trunk, then waved in Anna's direction as Will walked around the car to meet him, a new spring in his step.

They headed toward the school, where other students and fathers converged from different directions. Will was talking and laughing, and Austin laughed with him.

Anna watched them jealously until they disappeared inside the building. Then she drove to her office.

She stopped in at Austin Eats first, thinking that

caffeine and sugar might perk up her mood. She had
an appointment with new clients this morning and she
didn't want to rain on their wedding march.

"Hi!" Mary Jane called from behind the counter
as she took the coffeepot off the warmer. There was
not another soul in the restaurant. "I'm glad to see
you, Anna. I was beginning to feel like a character in
one of those movies where everyone else is dead.
They haven't bombed Texas, have they, and I'm the
only one who doesn't know?"

Anna had intended to get a cup of coffee to go, but
when Mary Jane headed toward the corner booth she
usually took, she followed her, thinking that a moment of peace and quiet had definite appeal.

"Yeah, but don't worry," Anna teased. "That
leaves all the chocolate in Texas for us."

Mary Jane laughed and poured coffee into both
cups on the table. Then she put the pot down and sat
opposite Anna.

"I guess we're all that's left of Austin's bachelor
girls. Or can you be a bachelor girl if you have a
child?"

Anna considered that while helping herself to a
napkin. "I think so. There was a movie called *Bachelor Father,* so I see no reason I can't be a bachelor
mother."

Her friend nodded. "Or me," she said, and took a
sip from her cup. Then she glanced at Anna with a
small smile, clearly waiting for a reaction.

"You?" Anna asked, eyes widening. "A...bach-
elor mother?"

Mary Jane nodded. "Yeah. I'm doing it for a friend

back east. Arielle was my nanny, and she and her husband haven't been able to conceive, so she asked me if I'd carry a baby for them. I'm excited.''

Anna wanted to smile, because Mary Jane was obviously happy. But in view of the emotional trauma of the past few days, her facial muscles seemed to be fighting her.

But no Maitlands ever cursed the world for what they couldn't have when their lives were otherwise so rich.

She smiled. ''Well, I'd be, too. Babies are wonderful, however they come. When are you due?''

''I'm not quite five months along.''

''And you don't even show. That's disgusting!''

Mary Jane patted her apron. ''This'll hide me for another few weeks, then I'll have to explain myself to everyone, I guess.''

''How's Sara?'' Anna asked. ''I thought she might be cooking today, but I see it's Joe.'' His bald head was visible through the window to the kitchen.

''She's taking care of personal business,'' Mary Jane replied. ''She got a loan for a new VW bug. She's happier than I've ever seen her.''

All right! Anna thought. At least she'd been able to make someone happy.

''I hear the Cahill-Lamont wedding is off.'' Mary Jane frowned. ''What happened? Who'd leave him? And why?''

Anna shrugged a shoulder and took a sip of coffee. ''The bride met an old flame and changed her mind.''

''Wow. Life's full of dirty tricks, isn't it?''

''Tell me about it.''

CHAPTER THIRTEEN

STAGE FRIGHT was a new experience for Austin. Over the span of his career, he'd spoken to rooms filled with stockholders, presided over meetings with hostile boards, explained changes in policy to his own employees and once even arbitrated a dispute between labor and management for a restaurant in one of his hotels.

But he'd never faced thirty-two fifth-graders who dared him to try to be more interesting than their own fathers, who also sat around the room.

Still, he'd promised Will, and thanks to his advertising team in Dallas, who'd put the program together for him, he had something he knew would please Will, if no one else.

Will introduced him, calling him with considerable, though flattering, exaggeration, "The smartest CEO in corporate America." The other children, who had no idea what corporate America was, were unimpressed.

But Will's teacher, Mrs. Watson, a pretty young blonde with a long braid and an ankle-length denim dress, smiled encouragingly as she closed the blinds to diminish the glare on the television screen for his presentation.

Austin thanked Will, watched the children wriggle in their seats and lose focus as he told them briefly about his company, his hotels and shopping malls. Then he put in the disk.

"We just bought RoyceCo," he explained while adjusting sound and clarity, "because the price of grain was high and I thought it was a good financial move to own a company that grew, stored and distributed grain. But it turned out that RoyceCo had a subsidiary company that's proven to be more interesting than the grain—a chain of pet stores."

Puppies romped across the screen, and the children laughed and sat up, their interest finally caught.

"I'd been prepared to sell Dogdom," he said as the camera closed in on one puppy at a time, catching silly antics. A dalmatian pup licked the camera lens, two teacup terriers rolled over and over in play, and a German shepherd with enormous ears posed liked a professional model. "Then Will told me that the company had been in trouble with the state of Texas because of animal protection violations—something I didn't even know. So I checked into it and found out that he was right."

The children aahed as a pile of five blond spaniels filled the screen.

"So I set up a puppy task force to go from store to store with a mobile veterinary unit to check and document the health of each puppy and treat those that require it."

A card appeared on the screen.

"Now each puppy has a card like this that tells us all about him or her, what shots he's had and which are due next. It'll tell a little bit about his personality and the qualities of the particular breed, so we might be able to guess what he'll be like as a full-grown dog. That helps us when a family comes looking for a dog to fill a certain need.''

The children were enraptured as the disk played on, showing more winsome puppies. A voice-over mentioned some of the breeds favored in Texas and explained their qualities while the appropriate pup frolicked with a member of the shop's staff. Austin stood back and let the rest of the video speak for itself.

He earned applause, congratulations from a father who was a veterinarian, for this responsible approach to assuming control of the pet shops and, when he and Will were alone in the back of the limo he'd hired to take them home, a heartfelt hug.

''You were the best!'' Will said with bright-eyed sincerity. ''The absolute best! Even better than Carrie Milton's dad, who's a stuntman for TV!''

''Thanks,'' he said, handing Will the other end of his seat belt. ''But I can't take all the credit. My advertising department made the disk for me.''

''But it was your idea,'' Will said, the old hero worship evident in his eyes. ''And you're the one who made sure the puppies would be taken care of. Are you gonna keep the company?''

''For a while,'' he said. ''Until we're sure the dogs are all well. Then I'll try to find the right buyer, so that we know they'll stay well.''

''That's so cool!''

As bright as Will's excitement was, it seemed to extinguish a moment later without warning.

"Now you're going back to Dallas?" Will asked.

"Not right away," he said, opening the bar and pouring Will a cola. "My mom's here, and she wants to spend a couple of days visiting friends. She just got back from a safari in Africa."

"Yeah?" Will's interest was sparked for a moment, then doused by the reality of their situation. "But you have to go, don't you? 'Cause even though you got Mom to say that she loves you, she can't have babies, and you really want one."

He'd have to teach the boy not to be so straightforward, Austin thought wryly, if he was going to make it in a boardroom when he grew up.

"Or is it because of me?" Will asked.

Austin didn't follow that logic. "I don't understand."

"Because if you want... What's it called? The reason you were gonna marry Miss Lamont?"

"An heir," Austin replied, looking at Will and thinking how the word paled in comparison to a *son*.

Will nodded gravely. "That's it. 'Cause an heir has to be your flesh and blood, right? And I'm...not."

Austin appreciated the guts that went into expressing such a thought—and risking the answer. It only confirmed for him the wisdom of the decision he'd made about three o'clock that morning.

"I've been thinking about this." Austin reached across the middle seat that separated them and put a hand to Will's shoulder. "I believe it's possible for a man to find a son and heir who isn't his own flesh and blood, but who's become part of his heart."

Will stared at him hopefully but warily, as though afraid he was misunderstanding.

"Like maybe a ten-year-old," Austin went on, giving his shoulder a small shake, "who's interested in all the same things and who'd be really fun to have around."

Will's unblinking eyes were filled with fireworks. "Me?" he asked on a whisper.

"Yeah," Austin replied. "What would you think of that?"

His answer was the flip of his seat belt and the flight of his body across the space that separated them and into Austin's arms.

Then Will raised his head worriedly. "But...Mom says you *can't* get married."

Austin hugged the boy to him. "I'll take care of your mother. But first we have to stop at my hotel. I have some friends I'd like you to meet."

ANNA DOODLED on a pad at her desk as dusk settled and traffic noises beyond her window rose with the after-work rush. She turned on her Art Nouveau tulip lamp for a closer look at the entwined hearts she'd created all over the page.

She ripped off the top sheet of her pad, squashed it in her hands and tossed it into the wastebasket, impatient with herself for emotional malingering.

If only Austin would stop off with Will so she could take her son home and try to resume life as it had been before Caroline Lamont hired her. Things had been simple then. Quiet and rather...flat, but simple.

Now her mind was so entangled, her heart so in pain she almost couldn't function.

She pushed impatiently away from her desk, heartache like a wound in her chest. She rubbed at it with her fingertips, heading toward the storeroom for her jacket and purse so she would be ready when Will arrived.

Austin wouldn't come up with him, she felt fairly certain. If he'd had any parting words for her, he'd have spoken them this morning.

In the stockroom, she stopped to square up a stack of boxes in the corner and heard the office door burst open.

"Mom!" Will's excited voice preceded his appearance in the small room. He was bright-eyed and flushed. "Mom! Look what I've got!"

"What—" she began to ask, then found the question unnecessary when Will thrust a coal-black puppy at her. It had floppy ears and big feet, and a tongue that flicked at her nose before she'd even taken it into her arms.

Will laughed hysterically while she was bathed with doggie kisses.

She felt the puppy's silky coat against her throat as it chewed at her hair. Will helped her free it, then the puppy went to work on the underside of her chin.

"Well," she said, and got a sloppy French kiss for her efforts. She rubbed a hand across her mouth while the puppy tried to climb her shoulder. "He certainly is...enthusiastic. Who does he belong to?"

"Me!" Will said gleefully. "Well, *us*. And he's a she. She's from Dogdom. Austin had her shipped to his hotel. Wait till you see what he did! He told us all about it at his presentation. He was the best dad there, Mom!''

The best dad there. She let herself pass right over that remark, knowing Will had simply misspoken in his excitement. ''I'm glad it went well. But...Will. A puppy.'' She was sure Austin had intended it as comfort for Will when he went back to Dallas, but she wished he'd discussed it with her first. ''I mean, we're gone all day.''

Will was absolutely aglow. ''But Rojalia's there, and Grandma Cahill is going to stay for a while to get to know us, so she'll be around to help.'' Then he suggested hopefully, ''Or we could get the puppy a friend.''

Grandma Cahill. Anna didn't really hear anything else. Will was apparently having as much trouble with emotional malingering as she was.

''Will,'' she said firmly. ''You don't have a grandma Cahill.''

''Oh, but he does.'' A slightly high-pitched but quiet voice corrected her.

Anna looked up to find a small, slender woman in a safari jacket standing in the storeroom's doorway. She had white hair, porcelain skin that was only slightly lined and tufty white hair that reminded her of Helen Hayes.

She stood on tiptoe to wrap Anna in a fragrant embrace. The puppy kissed her furiously. She laughed and stroked it, patted Anna's cheek.

''I'm Gloria Cahill, Austin's mother.''

Anna seemed to have lost all the air in her lungs.

"I'm...pleased to meet you," she said in a barely audible voice.

"She's been on safari!" Will said. "Now you can go on safari just to look, you don't shoot anything. She saw the lions in a game preserve and everything!"

"And I came home—" Gloria put an arm around Will's shoulders "—expecting to have to listen to plans for an outrageously staged ceremony commemorating Austin's deal with Caroline Lamont, and find instead that he's come to his senses." She smiled fondly. "Thank you so much for that."

Anna stared at her, thinking in a mild panic that she was hearing the words, but they refused to come together into a coherent thought. *Grandma* Cahill?

Then Austin's head and shoulders appeared behind his mother and Will as he put an arm around each of them.

"Do I have to come in there?" he asked doubtfully, his eyes scanning the small and already crowded dimensions of the stockroom, "or can we talk out here?"

"Why don't Will and I return to the hotel with Alice and reserve our table in the restaurant," Gloria said. "And you and Anna can come along when you're ready?"

"Alice?" Anna asked.

"The puppy," Will replied. "It's a nice soft name, like her."

"Good idea." Austin took the puppy from Anna and handed her to Will. "Just give her to the concierge. He said the desk clerks would watch him in the employees' lounge on their dinner break.''

"Okay.'' Will and Gloria hugged Austin, then Anna was alone with him in her suddenly very quiet office.

She was just beginning to understand his plan. He thought he could marry her anyway.

"I'm not going to let you do this,'' she said firmly, while inside her everything quaked. "It's a noble gesture you'll regret in a matter of months. You—''

She stopped abruptly when she saw the dangerous change take place in his eyes. She'd seen him angry the other night, during their argument, but that had been hot, passionate anger and somehow understandable.

This was cold, chin-squaring anger that seemed to affect even the way he moved. He advanced on her in an indolent, almost relaxed manner that she didn't trust for a moment.

She backed away. "Well, it is!'' she shouted at him. "I understand your wanting a baby! *I* want a baby! But I can't have one, so there's no point in pretending it doesn't matter, because it does!''

He had her trapped between his body and the escritoire in the corner. For one oddly exciting moment she had no idea what he intended to do. She told herself she didn't fear for her physical safety, yet at the same time he looked like a man at the absolute end of his patience.

Then he put his shoulder to her waist and straightened, clearing her feet off the ground and strapping an arm across the backs of her legs as she began to struggle.

"Austin Cahill!" she shouted. "What do you think you're doing?"

Whatever it was, he didn't feel obliged to answer. She heard a door open, then realized he'd walked into the storeroom. He set her on her feet and fixed her with that thunderous look that left her momentarily speechless.

"When you're ready to talk sense," he said with a calmness belied by his expression, "I'll let you out." He took two steps backward, then closed and locked the door.

Anna was imprisoned in her own storeroom.

She pounded once on the door. "This is ridiculous and juvenile!" she shouted.

"Yes, it is!" he shouted back. "But who forced me to resort to it?"

"Let me out!"

"When you stop talking idiocy!"

She went to the small step stool against the wall and sat down. If she thought she was going to plead for release, he had another think coming.

She waited.

And waited.

AUSTIN SAT at her desk, temper prodded beyond confining by that "noble gesture" remark. He propped his feet on her tidy desk blotter. He could sit here and wait as long as she could.

God, what a woman. He was probably crazy to try

to make her see the light. When she did and they got married, he'd be up against this behavior all the time.

It was a good thing his mother wasn't here to see his reaction to Anna. This was hardly the compromise she'd advised.

There was a rap on the storeroom door.

"Yeah?" he asked.

"How much oxygen do you estimate I have in here?" she demanded.

Though her question completely skirted the point he was trying to make, he gave her an answer. "Not enough to outlast me," he replied. "If you want to leave everything to Will, I'll pass on the information to your attorney."

"You're a heartless bully!"

"I didn't call your love a noble gesture."

There was a long silence, then she asked more quietly, "Will you please open this door?"

"No."

"But...I want to talk."

"Sense?" he demanded. "Or nonsense?"

A brief pause. "How can you talk sense," she asked, "when love is involved?"

"Whose love?"

Her indignant gasp was audible even through the door. "What do you mean *whose* love? Our love. Yours and mine."

"You mean your love and my noble gesture."

He heard a thunk, as though her forehead might have connected with the door.

"God, you're a bulldog! I know you love me, I

just don't want you to—to settle for less than you want.''

Settle. His temper hiked up a notch.

''When you croak in there,'' he called, ''I'm adopting Will.''

''All right!'' she shouted. ''I love you! Is that what you want to hear?''

''It's a start,'' he replied.

''What else?''

''I want to hear you retract the noble-gesture crack.''

''I'm sorry. I take it back.''

''And the settling-for-less-than-I-want remark.''

He heard the sigh. ''You completely misunderstand me!''

''No! You misunderstand *me!*''

There was a pause. ''Then I'm sorry,'' she said wearily. ''I'm sorry.''

She sounded on the brink of tears. Filled with remorse, though he still could have cheerfully throttled her, he opened the door.

She stood in the middle of the tiny room, arms folded, tears welling in her eyes. She gave him a condemning look then marched past him into the office. She stopped just behind him, and they turned to each other.

''All I meant,'' she said, her voice tremulous, ''was that I didn't think we could be happy if you weren't going to get what you wanted out of this relationship.''

He caught her arm and drew her to the fainting

couch in front of the window. "What do you think I want out of our relationship?" he asked.

She looked at him warily.

"It's not a trick question," he assured her. "Just answer it."

"A baby," she replied.

He shook his head. "That's what I wanted in my relationship with Caroline. The two of you aren't interchangeable to me, you know."

She frowned. "Then what *do* you want?"

"You and Will," he replied simply. "That's it."

A tear spilled over. "And you can just forget how much you want a baby?"

He didn't know how to explain that to her. He was just beginning to understand it himself. "I think I wanted a baby because I felt disconnected from everything important. I had money, status, *things,* but except for my mother, nobody belonged to me or me to them. So that was what I wanted from Caroline."

He ran a thumb across her cheek as another tear fell. "Then I began to love you, to feel your love for me. I saw the hero worship in Will's eyes—" he smiled thinly "—however misplaced, and suddenly I was connected. I felt secure in the universe."

Tears began to stream down her face, and she put a hand to her trembling mouth. "I wish I could have your baby," she cried.

He took her hand away, then framed her face in his palms and looked into her eyes. "I know. So do I. But it's something we can't have. And Will and I have decided that we're father and son even though we're not flesh and blood. So, if you can accept that, too, we've got it made.''

ANNA WRAPPED her arms around him and felt his arms enclose her. For a moment she wept into his shoulder and left all the old feelings of inadequacy slip away. Grievances ceased to exist. The future promised everything she'd ever wanted—for herself and for Will.

"If we want a baby somewhere down the road," he said, "I'm sure with your connections at Maitland Maternity, an opportunity will arise for private adoption." He laughed lightly. "Will says he wouldn't mind. He's in training to get ready for his cousin, anyway."

Anna squeezed him tightly and held on, her heart too full for speech.

Austin finally pushed her far enough away to reach into his hip pocket. He handed her a burgundy velvet box with a jeweler's name imprinted in gold.

"Oh, Austin," she said, taking it from him. "I don't need an engagement ring."

He shook his head. "That's not what it is."

Trying not to feel disappointed, she opened the box and stared at a band of pavé diamonds, with a two- or three-karat round-cut diamond in the center.

"I thought we'd skip the engagement," he said, taking it from the box and slipping it on her finger, "and go right to the wedding. Next weekend. What do you say? With all the doctors in your family, we should be able to get blood tests in time."

She threw her arms around him again, marveling

that in a life filled with blessings, she would be allowed this one, as well—love everlasting. She knew it would be. It had woven itself into the fibers of her being days ago.

"We'll have to write something into the vows about never locking me in a closet again."

He laughed. "It was a desperate gesture. I thought it would force you to listen to me. I love you," he said with sudden gravity. "And you and Will are all I need."

She leaned backward onto the couch and brought him with her until they lay face-to-face in each other's arms.

THERE WAS happiness in her eyes. He drank it in and felt it nourish him, as though he were some super being filled with wisdom and light.

"Where are we going to live?" she asked with practicality. "Will said something about your mom wanting to stay and get acquainted."

He traced her cheek with the knuckle of his index finger, fascinated by the delicate line of it. "I have a big place in Dallas and the ranch outside of San Antonio. When school's out, I'll take you to look at them. My office is in Dallas, but with today's technology, I can easily work from here. And Mom's always on the move anyway. She can use anywhere as home base."

Her eyes looked deeply into his, and he felt a moment's trepidation. There was something big on her mind, and he was almost afraid to hear it.

"You couldn't possibly imagine," she said in a

whisper, "how much I love you. It's made me forget everything bad, everything that hurts. All I know, all I feel is...happiness." She smiled, and with a sigh that seemed to signify trust and acceptance, leaned her weight against him and rested her head on his shoulder. "You're good, Austin. Really good."

He kissed her forehead and held her even closer. "Wait until you see what the three of us can do together."

* * * * *

MAITLAND MATERNITY
continues with
HER BEST FRIEND'S BABY
by
Vicki Lewis Thompson

Irrepressible Mary Jane Potter figured she owed Arielle big time for years of being big sister, mother substitute and best friend in the whole world. Doing something major was the only way to settle the debt, and carrying a child for Arielle and her husband, Morgan, qualified. But the world tilted when Morgan Tate came to Austin with devastating news that would change all their lives...forever.

Available next month
Here's a preview!

CHAPTER ONE

MORGAN COULD SEE that Mary Jane was very good at what she did. More than good. An artist. He sensed the creative energy going into her work as she made his sundae. And watching her was an erotic experience for him. As she ladled on the thick fudge sauce, it slid down between the plump mounds of vanilla, melting the ice cream as it went. It occurred to him that warm, sticky chocolate would make a good body paint.

He couldn't believe he was having thoughts like that. Kinky had never been a part of his repertoire, but spending time with Mary Jane was bringing out all sorts of hidden facets in his personality. He had a feeling she would be willing to get messy in order to have some fun.

Then she picked up the can of whipping cream. As she squirted it in an artful pyramid, he had no trouble picturing her putting that can to great use on a certain part of his anatomy. And then she'd have to lick it off....

Depraved. That's exactly what he was becoming, and he needed to get control of himself. Mary Jane needed someone to watch out for her welfare, not someone to dream up exotic love scenes with her as the focal point.

"There you go." She set the sundae on the counter in front of him and gave him a long-handled spoon.

He admired the symmetry of the whipped cream, the blend of brown fudge and vanilla ice cream showing through the clear sides of the glass, the even sprinkling of nuts on top of the clouds of whipping cream, the bright red cherry sitting perfectly balanced on top. "It's so beautiful I hate to eat it," he said, glancing at her.

She looked incredibly proud of herself. "You have to eat it. It tastes even better than it looks."

"I'll bet." But he was thinking about her, not the ice cream treat. Her expression was so adorable he wished he could snap a picture to keep with him.

"Here's your lunch, Mary Jane," Sara called, putting a plate on the pass-through. "Heavy on the lettuce."

"Thanks, I think." Mary Jane took the plate and put it on the counter next to where Morgan was sitting. Then she came around the counter and slid onto the stool beside him. "You haven't taken a single bite!"

"I was waiting for you."

"Well, I'm here. Dig in!"

He was aware of her gaze on him as he pushed the spoon into the sundae, getting it far enough in to reach some of the fudge. Bringing up a dripping spoonful, he put it in his mouth. Then he closed his eyes with pleasure. It tasted like Mary Jane's kiss.

"Good, huh?" she asked eagerly.

He opened his eyes. She sat there anticipating his certain praise, and her face looked as if it were lit from within. He'd never had anyone look so happy about creating something special just for him, and his throat closed at the sweetness of it.

As he looked into her sparkling eyes, the truth came over him. He wasn't going to get over Mary Jane. Not in a few weeks, not in a few months, not ever. She'd taken up residence in his heart.

"I'll bet it's so wonderful, you're having trouble finding the words to describe it," she said. "Sometimes my customers are speechless with delight over my hot fudge sundaes."

He cleared the hoarseness from his throat and smiled at her. "That's exactly my problem," he said. "I'm speechless."

"I knew it. Eat up. It'll fix whatever ails you."

He didn't think so.

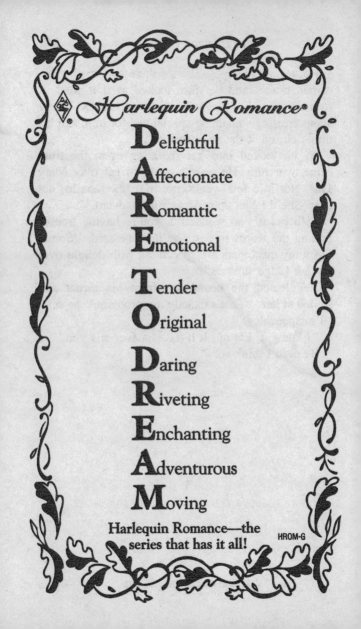

Harlequin Romance®

Delightful

Affectionate

Romantic

Emotional

Tender

Original

Daring

Riveting

Enchanting

Adventurous

Moving

Harlequin Romance—the
series that has it all!

HROM-G

HARLEQUIN ◆ PRESENTS®

The world's bestselling romance series...
The series that brings you your favorite authors,
month after month:

Helen Bianchin...Emma Darcy
Lynne Graham...Penny Jordan
Miranda Lee...Sandra Morton
Anne Mather...Carole Mortimer
Susan Napier...Michelle Reid

and many more uniquely talented authors!

Wealthy, powerful, gorgeous men...
Women who have feelings just like your own...
The stories you love, set in exotic, glamorous locations...

HARLEQUIN PRESENTS,
Seduction and passion guaranteed!

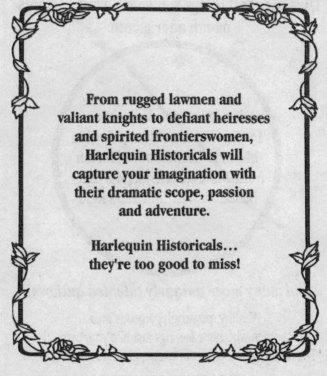

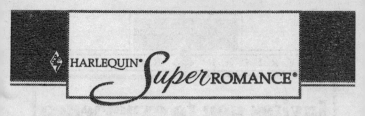

...there's more to the story!

Superromance.
A *big* satisfying read about unforgettable characters. Each month we offer *six* very different stories that range from family drama to adventure and mystery, from highly emotional stories to romantic comedies—and much more! Stories about people you'llbelieve in and care about. Stories too compelling to put down....

Our authors are among today's *best* romance writers. You'll find familiar names and talented newcomers. Many of them are award winners— and you'll see why!

If you want the biggest and best in romance fiction, you'll get it from Superromance!

Available wherever Harlequin books are sold.

HARLEQUIN®
Makes any time special.™

Upbeat, all-American romances about the pursuit of love, marriage and family.

Two brand-new, full-length romantic comedy novels for one low price.

Rich and vivid historical romances that capture the imagination with their dramatic scope, passion and adventure.

Sexy, sassy and seductive— Temptation is hot sizzling romance.

A bigger romance read with more plot, more story-line variety, more pages and a romance that's evocatively explored.

Love stories that capture the essence of traditional romance.

Dynamic mysteries with a thrilling combination of breathtaking romance and heart-stopping suspense.

Meet sophisticated men of the world and captivating women in glamorous, international settings.